Olga Nazimov by W. L. George

TO MY FRIEND SHEILA KAYE-SMITH

Walter Lionel George was born to British parents on 20th March 1882 in Paris, France.

It was not until he was a young man of 20 that he learned English. In 1905 he moved to London to work in an office but soon found himself working as a journalist, as a foreign correspondent, for various London newspapers.

By 1911, with the publication of his first novel 'A Bed of Roses', which portrayed the fall of a penniless young woman into prostitution, his efforts were rewarded and he turned to literature as a full time career.

His writings now sold well. He added short stories to his offerings as well as literary essays and several tracts that discussed left-wing themes. Others thought his subject matter to be difficult and poorly chosen and his political views gained him little credit amongst his peers although such luminaries as George Orwell praised both subject matter and style.

His personal life was also turbulent. His three marriages left him widowed twice. In 1908 he married Helen Porter who died in 1914, Helen Agnes Moorhead followed in 1916 but she died in 1920. His last marriage was to Kathleen Geipel in 1921.

W. L George died on 30th January 1926.

Index of Contents

OLGA NAZIMOV

Chapter I

Already the few passengers had dispersed in groups owning many children who, proudly assured, wrangled for the privilege of carrying hat-boxes, baskets of groceries or of fish. Solitary women passed, also laden with packages, while here and there stalked by a tall and corpulent official in uniform anxious to ignore his umbrella or his fishing-rod. For a moment John Hulder stood looking beyond the broken-down old carriage, in every corner of which, save a little space for him, was piled his neat American luggage. In the blaze of August light, under the crashing purple of the sky, his possessions seemed to stare, the brass bindings of his trunks and their scarlet lettering to have gained violence of colour and of form in the blazing air of the Swiss summer.

Though this was a weekday, Ammenzell was not sleepy as would have been an Italian town. There was an air of business about the little fruit-shop and its show of apricots, peaches and ruddy apples; about the post office with perpetually active doors under the republican scutcheon; about the terrace of the Hotel de Paris, where sat a few middle-aged tourists before steaming coffee or tall mugs of pale beer. A glow of heat seemed to seize Hulder, to penetrate through the loose grey flannels to his skin. He had a sensation of well-being, for this heat was less than the one he had just left in Tyrol. And yet it left him so limp that he started when at last the coachman bent toward him a sunburnt old face with an enormous grizzled moustache and asked, "Where does the gentleman wish to drive?"

Hulder did not reply for a moment, for he did not know what he wanted to do. He looked about him, wondered whether he should put up at the Hotel de Paris or select its rival, the Royal. But both of these, facing south-west, looked intolerably stuffy. In his good, precise French he questioned the coachman, pointing to the little hills above the town.

The driver was not uncertain. Excitedly pointing with his whip, he declared that not much more than a mile off was a wonderful hotel, the National.

"Well," said Hulder briefly, with the sharpness of the irresolute taking a decision, "to the National then."

As he sank down into the dusty cushions, and the horse began to move with immense deliberation, he wondered what he was doing at Ammenzell and what he wanted to do. It did not look like an exciting place. No doubt on Sundays it would be gay enough if he wanted to be gay.

As brightness fell from the air, Hulder found himself weary. A Bostonian, aged about thirty, he had studied the law because his parents considered that he ought to apologize to the United States for not having to earn a living. His apology made and his parents dead, he had found out little by little that the quiet solitudes of Boston bored him as much as the occasionally feverish agitation of its copper market.

He had found the West too large and too rough, New York too shrill; for a moment the peace of Georgian England transplanted into Louisiana had held him, but only for a moment. In Louisiana he realized by contrast that there was very little room in America for a man with nothing to do. He only wanted to live.

As a natural consequence of this feeling he had sailed for Europe, and had for a while been charmed by the capacity of the older races to do nothing with wonderful, sleepy intentness. And so, for two years, he had progressed round the Continent from London, its Trafalgar Square hotels, its Chelsea salons, to Paris and its hysterical glitter, to sturdy Berlin trying so hard to be vicious and gloomily conscious that it was born respectable. It had not been very adventurous: he had wandered in Spain and encountered nothing worse than insects; he had ridden across the Abruzzi without being held to ransom by brigands and, even in Russia, he had never been suspected of advanced ideas. And so he was a little disappointed in the romance of life as he lay back in the old carriage that now crawled up the hill at less than a foot pace, the horse impatiently biting at the flies, first on his right shoulder, then on his left. Hulder reflected upon this: the double strain in his temperament, this strange desire to take no active part in life, and this hope that something outside him would happen to stimulate that life and make it vivid.

"I don't think it's going to be very vivid here," he remarked aloud to himself. "I ought to have known better than ask that waiter."

This opinion was strengthened as the carriage passed between the elaborate villas of the Geneva merchants, then over the gaily painted bridge that spanned the little river, by the palisades beyond which were the trim gardens bursting with clematis and night primroses. Yes, that Geneva waiter who, in reply to Hulder's question as to whether there were in the neighbourhood some beautiful country places where it would not be too hot, had named Ammenzell, might have been happy enough here, but—Hulder sighed. After all, what did it matter? Haste or sloth, it was much the same in the end.

Now they were well above the little town. Turning back, he could see the villas clustering on the slopes down to the edge of the lake. Truculent, among them stood the Chateau, no doubt the centre of government, and the church with the red-tiled roof and the amazing swelling in the middle of the spire that looked exactly like a large onion. A pleasant place enough, especially that day when no colour could shrink into greyness under the enormous pummelling of the sun.

A turn of the road, a little downhill, the scraping of the brakes—that made Hulder smile, for he was not yet accustomed to drivers who never control a horse by means of the reins then again flatness, the horse suddenly inspired by insults to arrive in style—the coachman turning in his seat, pointing with his whip toward a large solitary building. Among the rumble of the wheels Hulder could distinguish only the word "National." He nodded languidly, and yet was amused to feel some slight excitement: a new name, a new place, there was always something exciting in that. He smiled, wondered whether this proved him more American than he knew.

Within half-an-hour Hulder was in possession of his new quarters, a bedroom on the second floor, to which was attached a little sitting-room abutting on a balcony. Far below him lay the valley. Beyond the Chateau, its girdling dales and the church, which he christened St. Onions, lay the lake, and beyond that, sharply outlined like grey lace, the length of peaks of the distant Alp. A content rilled him, for this landscape had nobility. A sense of eternity was about it: he could feel that there had always been an Alp, that the Alp would endure for ever, and for a second he was glad that he had come to Geneva's Sunday playground, to this singular National. For the National was indeed a curious place; its august name notwithstanding, sheds and stables showed that it had once been a farm. Rising a little in the world, it had turned into an inn; then two storeys had been added, four cupolas had been built on the corners, and the whole had been painted a delicate shade of salmon pink relieved at every moulding in vermilion. The front garden, half covered by an awning for bad weather, was occupied by little tables at which, most hours of the day, a countryman in Swiss national costume, a ruck-sacked tourist or a forester could be seen slowly eating and drinking. The National was homely, and even its unexpected ostentations, its self-recommendation in the shape of automobile and cycle club boards, failed to make it anything but homely. As the afternoon dragged on, and very slowly the sun began to sink, spreading gold and purple over the mountains and darkening to black the dull waters of the lake, Hulder felt more keenly the oppression of the place.

The inhabitants of the hotel did not seem thus oppressed. There were a good many of them, mainly women and children sent to take the air while husbands and fathers worked in Geneva until the Saturday afternoon. Long before supper-time, when Hulder had aimlessly gone in and out of the hotel to walk through the steep meadows to the church and to see the abominable frescoes and ornaments of which it was so proud, he had realized this. There was a young girl, in a dress of blue print spattered with bunches of red and green flowerets, in charge of two little girls; there was a newly married couple, she very small and dark, he very handsome, very fair, and showing a strip of milk-white calf above the short grey woollen socks which he wore in fanciful imitation of the Swiss peasant; there was an old gentleman who looked like a retired general and was probably a post office official having a fortnight's holiday; and there were children. Children! The National, Hulder thought, was nothing but a creche. It contained quite twenty children, fortunately quiet, respectable Swiss children who knew that most things were defendues, and made no attempt to do them, but, to the end of his stay, Hulder never quite found out to whom they belonged. Some of them, a maid told him within an hour of his arrival, belonged to Madame Pettinger, on the first floor, but as there seemed to be a perpetual circulation of children between the various apartments, and as the Pettingers had but two rooms, it was quite impossible to tell whether the abundant lady housed a dozen of her own or merely held out to all small creatures an affectionate, large red hand.

No, it was not very promising. Quite apart from the fact that the whole of the premises was intimately pervaded by a curious and pungent smell, almost certainly lavender, the supper which was offered Hulder at seven o'clock was as bad as any he had ever refused in an Italian town. It was worse: in the old days in America, when he was liberal-minded, he had not believed in the fondness of the Swiss for pig; he now had to confess that this was no fable, for the menu of the National seemed compounded entirely with allotropic forms of the animal. Also there was red cabbage, fiercely vinegary. And a fruit tart, the massive dough of which could have served as a rock on which to rear the ambition of a new faith. Alone the perfect iced wine, like pale sunshine, enabled Hulder to get through his meal. His companions at the long table did not amuse him much. He had been placed at this because he was alone. The little tables were occupied by parties, and at his own were mainly the solitaries of the hotel: the old official, a middle-aged couple as large as the Pettingers but childless, two valiantly touristic young men, an elderly lady and, by his side, a young woman to whom he at first paid very little attention, so exasperated was he by the badness of the food, and so hypnotized by the way in which an old gentleman juggled with his knife and pieces of meat.

Suddenly the young woman at his side spoke. He started and as, in reply to the remark he had not understood, he said, "Pardon?" he looked at her. He saw a rather strange face, which he vaguely summed up as foreign. He observed very black hair and large, steady grey eyes under high-arched brows. No more, for his neighbour explained that she wanted salt. He handed it to her, observed the great length and fineness of her hands, the skin of which had an unusual dead-white quality. She thanked him, bent down toward her plate, averted her head a little as if to show that she had no wish to carry the conversation any further. As the dinner went on, very long and not rendered less wearisome by the chatter from every table, and the occasional shrillness of children's voices that came from the amalgamated company of infants whom Madame Pettinger seemed to control, Hulder found himself watching his neighbour and hoping that she would turn her face toward him. He had seen enough to know that hers was an interesting countenance. Little by little, by craning forward and quickly looking sideways, he discovered that there was hardly any colour in the dead white of her cheeks, that her mouth was small, very red, purplish, and rather pouting. But he observed another peculiarity, a very sharply pointed chin, and something which he did not at once realize, but was a Scotch height of cheekbones. A little later in the meal he was able to offer her another condiment, was thanked, ventured to suggest that the room was oppressively hot. She agreed without looking up. And when, a little later, determined to make her look at him, he dropped his napkin and picked it up, apologizing as he did so, the large grey eyes rested upon him only for a moment, and almost as if they did not see him but were occupied with some other object invisible to him, clear to them.

She rose early from the table and, as Hulder's eyes followed her to the window, he was conscious of something peculiar in her attitude. She was rather short, broad-shouldered, full-bosomed; there was about her something reposeful and self-reliant. He guessed her to be twenty-five or six. And now, as she looked through the window toward the darkling sky in which still flamed the last lights of a rutilant sunset, she seemed concentrated and intent. Quite intimately Hulder knew that she was waiting for somebody, and he was surprised, as his mind leapt to husband or lover, to find himself touched by disappointment. Why should he be disappointed? Why should he be in the least interested in the relations of a casual neighbour?

No doubt, he thought next day, it was because Ammenzell did not appear likely to yield him much interest. There had been a storm in the night, and now it was cooler. He had walked down to the lake, been pestered by boatmen to row or sail; he had read the Journal de Geneve; he had bought a peach. Nothing had happened, and at lunch the place by his side was empty. Cautious inquiries from the serving-maid drew out that his neighbour's name was Nazimov, that she was a Russian, and that she had that day gone to Geneva to meet her brother who was coming to stay at the hotel. A satisfaction came to Hulder out of these details. A brother, he thought, was better than either husband or lover. Then he laughed at himself; as he walked, puffing at his pipe, through the flower-spangled meadows that lay right and left of the road to Starnois, he told himself not to be a fool. That evening, when again the place beside him was empty, he saw that Miss Nazimov was seated at a little table with a strange, slight young man whose features were as elastic as her own seemed rigid; yet he could not escape his feeling of disappointment. It translated itself into emotion. Often he found himself looking toward the table, but his glance never crossed with that of Miss Nazimov. He could see her lips slowly moving as she talked, but she did not raise her eyes toward him; all that he could do was to admire the length of the long black lashes that made a shadow on her cheeks. More often his eyes met those of the young man, for these were roving, active, as if his curiosity were continually stimulated, and as if nothing that he saw could satisfy it. Two or three times during dinner he looked at the American, and Hulder was amused, also perhaps a little disquieted by the variations of the young man's expression: most of his glances were casual, but once Hulder thought that the young man smiled at him, while, just before he stood up to go outside and smoke over his coffee, he was sure that he could trace upon his features an expression of extreme malevolence.

It was all, he thought as he went out, rather curious, and therefore rather interesting. He wondered whether these people would not prove disappointing, as so many had done in so many European hotels. Still, he was glad to be even so far interested.

Chapter II

"What are you staring at?"

Hulder turned round suddenly at the sound of the high, not unmelodious voice, which he instinctively knew to be that of the peculiar young man. He hardly knew how to reply to the unceremonious question, and his embarrassment was not lessened by the sharp, half-truculent tone in which it had been couched, nor by the young man's strange appearance. He could see him distinctly enough in the strong light of the two lamps which surmounted the gate of the National. He was about the same height as his sister, but much slighter, and Hulder observed, almost with amusement, that he very closely resembled her: black hair, arched eyebrows, large grey eyes, pointed chin, all the features were alike, but an untidy mass of hair fell over the young man's left eye; a little black moustache continually moved, as if the lip from which it grew were nervously twitching. And the grey eyes were not steady but anxious, questioning. The general impression in the American's mind, one of nervous weakness, was carried out by his companion's unexpected clothing. Over a jacket, which he now saw was velvet, fell the rough folds of a frieze cape; from the loose, soft collar flowed a black silk tie, so untidily knotted that one end had leapt from the waistcoat. And, ridiculous to think, as the young man stood, the coat outspread because his hands were resting on his hips, Hulder was reminded of a large, excited crow.

"Well," repeated the young man, a little angrily, "what are you staring at?"

His French was almost faultless, but still rather peculiar.

"Staring at? " said Hulder vaguely, taking the cigar from his teeth. "I don't know. The moon." He nodded toward the horizon.

The young man took a step towards him, leant against the parapet which separated the garden from the road.

"Ah! " he murmured. "The moon."

For a moment his gaze fixed upon the planet, which hung very low in a dark blue sky, the blue-black sky of the Southern heavens in the late evening. Against this deep screen the moon floated like a brilliant orange lamp, rather as a glowing circle of wedded yellow, orange and salmon pink. Hulder was no longer looking at the moon, but at the young man rapt in contemplation, as if adoring.

"The moon!" repeated the young man. "Yes, she's worth staring at. She's one of the eternal things. She makes one believe in eternity, because it's so hard to think that one thing can be eternal and not another. It is so difficult to believe in eternity, don't you think?"

"I don't know," said Hulder confusedly. "They teach us that we shall live again and—"

"Tush," said the young man angrily.

"Well," said Hulder, "I haven't thought much about eternity, you see."

There was a long pause, during which a variety of expressions succeeded one another upon the young man's features.

"No," he said. Then, very slowly, "I suppose a man like you wouldn't think much about eternity. You don't need to. No, you don't need to," he repeated more loudly, as Hulder raised a protesting hand to show that he disliked the imputation of thoughtlessness. "You don't need to because death for you is so far away that you never think of it, while I—"

He paused, and Hulder felt disquieted in the presence of impending revelation. The young man's tone changed. Hulder thought of a swerving horse.

"Fiodor Kyrilovitch Nazimov. And you?"

Hulder gathered that the young man had introduced himself.

"John Hulder," he said briefly. "That's my name."

He sought for some commonplace topic, but Nazimov forestalled him.

"John Hulder," he repeated. "Oh, I knew you were English when I saw you. That's why you never think of eternity."

Hulder smiled. "Perhaps the English don't," he said. "But I might, because, you see, I'm American. You're wrong, you see, Fiodor Kyrilovitch."

A smile creased Nazimov's mouth as he heard the familiar appellation. "Oh!" he said. "You know how to address a Russian! You know Russia? "

"Yes," said Hulder, "a little."

"H'm," said Nazimov sulkily, "you know Russia!"

"Yes."

"I suppose you know it like all Americans. Samovars, vodka, Tolstoy, Russian dances, the knout and the Czar—" He suddenly broke into excellent English. "And all that sort of rot."

"Oh!" said Hulder, amused, though his tone was offensive. "You speak English, too?"

"Yes," said Nazimov. "I was in England some years. There was no other place to go to after I had said that the Grand Duchess Antonia dyed her hair, or something like that."

"So you're a Nihilist," said Hulder, laughing.

"One doesn't become a Nihilist because one says that a Grand Duchess dyes her hair," Nazimov replied, laughing, too. "Still, it's very awkward in Russia if one says that sort of thing."

Just as Hulder was opening his mouth to resume the conversation, Nazimov turned away from him and again began to gaze at the high-hung 'fiery pan of the moon, as if he had forgotten all about the American.

"The moon," he murmured. "Single eye of a Cyclops with a dark blue brow—too far away for anything but tolerance, too cold to warm, too selfish to do anything save steal such warmth as it can from the sun, too feminine to give off any light save that which it reflects from a brighter star hateful, abominable, loathsome moon." His tone changed, suddenly became thoughtful. "And yet, there is no moon and no earth, no moon save in the imagination of men who think there are such things. Life is but a dream, the nightmare of some giant sleeping in the void and I the soul of that giant, wandering while he sleeps, haunted by phantoms and phantasies. It is I, that flying soul, whose distraught imagination creates star and moon and man and Hotel National for him to dwell in; and when he and I have dreamed long enough, and we awake because I dream no more for him, I, the giant, shall be no more. I, the dreamer, am only a dream."

He paused, and there was a long silence while Hulder struggled to piece together in his mind such philosophy as remained to him from his college course. He understood Nazimov, and a faint memory of Berkeley came to him, but he was deflected from this purely intellectual exercise by the interest aroused in him by the passion, half of pain and half of anger, that was in Nazimov's voice. And then, quite suddenly, while he was wondering what to reply to the extraordinary tirade, he heard from the hotel steps a cry of, "Fedia!"

Nazimov's features became alert. He cried out something in Russian and, at once, running down the steps, Hulder saw the sister. She came toward them with swift, long steps, and Hulder was struck by her expression, half-anxious, half-angry, by the chiding, disdainful tone in which she addressed her brother, and the dominating, motherly way in which she wound round his neck and mouth a knitted red and green comforter. She was still, Hulder gathered from her tone, expostulating with him, and Hulder, guessing from Nazimov's thin frame that he was delicate and should not stand in the open at night, threw out a few words of apology. At once the girl turned on him.

"How could you do such a thing? " she asked in French. "Can't you see he's delicate?"

"I'm sure I'm very sorry," said Hulder.

"Sorry!" she repeated scornfully. "I'd have thought that you'd have had more sense than that. Come along, Fedka; you must have something hot and go to bed."

"To bed at half-past nine? " said Nazimov, smiling. "Oh, Olichka, you can't mean that, my first night; and I've been enjoying myself with Mr. Hulder."

"Have you?" said the girl more gently. She threw Hulder a glance in which was less hostility, but merely doubt. "I'm glad you've had a nice talk. But really, Fedichka, you must be careful, and Mr.—Mr.—"

"Hulder," said Nazimov. . . . "This is my sister, Olga Kyrilovna."

She bowed a little stiffly, and for a second Hulder wished that he were not too self-conscious to follow the Russian custom. He would have liked to bend down and kiss that long fine hand. But Nazimov and his sister were not shy. Now that Olga realized her brother's pleasure in the American's company, a change seemed to have come over her. She smiled, and her teeth were beautiful.

It was a peculiar atmosphere they made, these two, as they laughed, nestled against each other, chattered excitedly in soft, bell-like Russian, or broke into French, or, for his benefit, into English. Olga had apparently forgotten her anger. Her mood had changed swift as the cloud which fleeted as a film of blue gauze across the molten gold of the moon. But she was still watching over her brother, compelling him to draw close the wings of the cape, and winding more tightly over his mouth the length of the comforter. At last she once more declared that Fiodor must go to bed. As she took him away, they were laughing. And again, an hour later, when Hulder met her in the hall as she carried a glass of hot milk, when he bade her "Good-night," she smiled at him.

"You know," she said confidentially, "Fiodor seems to like you."

"Oh, so do I like him," said Hulder, a little awkwardly, for outspoken emotion disturbed him.

"I'm so glad," said Olga. "You know," she added seriously, "he isn't very well. I must be very careful."

Chapter III

It was perhaps because Hulder felt little interest in his fellow-guests that he concentrated upon the Nazimovs. It is true that, on the second day, the retired official had taken him apart to tell him that it was a pity Switzerland had no Bismarck to deal with the Socialists; and Madame Pettinger had asked him whether he was married and had children, adding, as a rider to his reply, some surprised and disapproving remarks because he was neither a husband nor a father. But there was something more appealing, because more mysterious, about the young Russians. More and more they appeared to Hulder as lovers rather than as brother and sister, and he was not surprised to find that they were twins; their similarity of feature was proof enough. But Olga seemed a mother as well as a sister; while Fiodor liked to leave the hotel with Hulder, or to stand alone at the edge of the creeper-grown quarry near by, there apparently to meditate, Olga was agitated when she did not see him. Suddenly, in the midst of a conversation, her look would wander; she would become curiously thoughtful, brooding; her eyes would shine with entranced intensity. And, quite as suddenly, without even a word of apology, she would leap up from her seat, and Hulder could hear her run up the stairs, or across the gravel in the front garden, as if she were anxious and seeking. And she watched over Fiodor materially as well as emotionally, sometimes to his annoyance, often to his amusement. When she swaddled him up in the comforter, or demanded for him the liver wing of a chicken, or practically lifted him out of his chair and into another because there was a draught, Fiodor would throw his American friend a humorous glance of self-pity. But, on the whole, theirs was a relation of tender intimacy: seldom did they address each other as Olga or Fiodor; it was always Fedia or, more tenderly, Fedichka; and he caressingly called her Olichka, sometimes, in a soft, melting voice, Olusha. The Russian diminutives, expressive of all grades of love, dallying or anger, were their everyday language. Tender they were, both of them, though sometimes combative and angry, when it was the contemptuous Fedka or Olka came, sharp and vengeful.

Hulder was now their chosen companion. On the third morning Fiodor came to him, laid upon the table two beautiful longhands, and gazed at him with immense, pathetic grey eyes. Hulder looked up, smiling, waiting for some poetic thought, and Fiodor said—

"This place smells like a dustheap; come with us into the town."

Before Hulder could reply, Olga joined them. Her face was impassive, but she looked at her brother, at his animated eyes, and a sweet, slow smile lit up her features. They walked down the hill, those three, Fiodor talking all the time, ramblingly, sometimes profound, then suddenly commonplace, but always nervously intent.

"See, there are the mountains, there just beyond the pines, blue to-day—no, grey-blue like the wing of a heron—that's the Wetterspitze—three thousand metres high, so Baedeker says." He laughed. "Why don't they label the mountains—with their height and" (a wicked smile at Hulder) "with their price delivered post free in New York State?"

"Oh, we don't buy mountains," said Hulder; "we've got as many as we want."

They laughed together. Fiodor stuck to his point. "Our mountains are more historic than the Rockies. Don't laugh, Hulder; one of your millionaires will buy the St. Bernard district one day and transplant it to Ohio, and build a house on it and call it Napoleon Villa."

Then, before Hulder could reply, Fiodor was being jocular at the expense of little Ammenzell, which they were now entering. All three, that morning, felt very young, ready to be amused by the villas of the Geneva merchants, their extraordinary roofs copied from those of pagodas, and the delightful alliance of the Swiss chalet with the Spanish colonnade. Indeed, it was a humorous district, for one very rich merchant had been carried away by his business instincts: at the wrought-iron gates of his summer palace, beyond which spangled rose bushes and passionate clematis fought for predominance, some ungovernable impulse had compelled him to put up a large board advertising that his name was Holtzen, and that his bath fittings were the greatest in the world.

The talk was all Fiodor's, for Hulder tried vainly to draw Olga into conversation; in his presence she seemed to want to remain silent. She was courteous, she replied, she smiled, but it could not be said that she talked. Eye and hand, she was bound to her brother, and tactfully so, for when, at a short hill, she murmured to Fiodor, "Give me your arm, Fedia," Hulder observed that, unobtrusively, she did not hang upon that arm, but supported it.

They shopped. At the bootmaker's there was a cheerful scene, for Olga, who wanted sandals, found it quite impossible to fit her long, arched foot into the shoes destined for the ladies of Geneva. Not a shoe that was not three sizes too broad, if it fitted her length! And she smiled a little proudly when Hulder suggested that none save a bootmaker who had made for greyhounds could hope to fit her slenderness.

They bought those things that tourists need: picture postcards, newspapers, cigarettes of a special brand for Fiodor. Hulder would have been filled with satisfaction if, at the post office, something had not happened. Quite suddenly, in the midst of the sunlit street, Fiodor stopped. He choked; his face reddened, and then, with his sister's arm about his shoulders, he was coughing, coughing horribly, as if the spasm tore at something deep in his body. While his eyes still stared, Olga pressed her handkerchief against his mouth. For a moment Hulder lost sight of the convulsed face as Olga's strong shoulders turned towards him, but he had time to see, when at last the coughing subsided, that there was blood upon the handkerchief.

Hulder stood by them, anxiously. Fiodor threw the American a very soft smile, said something in a whisper which made Olga's features into a rigid white mask.

"What?" asked Hulder. "What do you say, Fiodor Kyrilovitch?"

Olga raised her hand, but already and quite loud, Fiodor, still smiling, had said, "143."

"Hush! Hush!" came Olga's low voice. "For shame, Fedichka, how can you say such things? It isn't true."

"It is true, Olusha," murmured Fiodor, "but what does it matter? Come, Hulder, I'm strong enough to walk up the hill."

As the American accompanied them towards the National, he was wondering and charmed. Puzzled by this incomprehensible figure, 143, and the effect it had, he was charmed by the glowing tenderness that had been in Olga's voice. He could not shake off the impression, even though, in half-an-hour, he was playing a game of billiards with Fiodor. He played well, the Russian badly. Olga, her hands folded in her lap, watched them from a window, smiling, her gaze upon the American, very gentle and responsive to every one of her brother's words. But Fiodor was quite outclassed. Already Hulder had made thirty-five to his eight. The young Russian flung down his cue and, without a word, walked away. In the same minute Olga stood up, and Hulder went up to her with a smile upon his face, as if inviting her to sympathize with him because her brother was behaving like a naughty child. But he drew back in amazement: Olga's mouth had set into a straight line, her black eyebrows into a savage knot; giving him but a single look of contained rage, she turned her back upon him.

Chapter IV

As an overladen ship that tumbles groaning from the crest to the trough of waves, the strange friendship progressed. Had these three not been intellectually isolate among the tourists, it would have suffered disaster, so angry and uncertain was the intercourse that built it. Hulder was never easy with the Russians: nothing told him that some chance word would not arouse their rage or, worse still, a crooning fondness translating itself into prayers that he would forgive. The atmosphere was hectic, and his friends were mantled in mystery; shockingly, Fiodor had, on the previous night, seen him come towards him upon the road, then, with a high, crackling laugh, cried out "141," and rushed away towards the quarry.

The incomprehensible figure bit into Hulder's imagination. The original "143" was now "141"—and two days had elapsed. He groped for significances, for some object Fiodor aimed at, attainable only with the efflux of time. But he doubted his own capacity to follow into some unguessed cavern the will-o'-the-wisps of Fiodor's thoughts. And now, still anxious, but too well-bred to question him, he lay upon the moss in the little wood, at the feet of the young Russian, who sat propped up against a tree-trunk.

"How beautiful it is! " he said at last.

Indeed, all things were beautiful in that minute, the tall, slim trunks of the pines, gilded and empurpled with sunshine, the brown-violet bed of needles, the patches of flowered meadows, yellow-green, that rolled up to a distant hill. And the silence, seldom pierced by the call of a bird. His long hands languid upon the moss, his eyes high-raised, Fiodor seemed not to have heard. But he replied, relevantly enough—

"Beauty—the great anodyne I Immortality, absolute, therefore beautiful . . ." His voice sank into a murmur as if he thought aloud. "Yes, true enough, naught save two anodynes to this long disease they call life philosophy and art: philosophy that transcends life, and art that illumines it. Life might be lived if . . ."

The murmur became a cry; his face was convulsed. "If it were true!" he shouted. "If there were anodynes! Liar! Do you hear, Hulder! Schopenhauer is a liar; there are no anodynes. Listen," he went on, speaking quickly, low, as a child revealing a secret: "there are no anodynes for life unless you imagine there are anodynes. There is nothing that makes life bearable except the illusion that one enjoys it. It is in our hands to dream as we will, and to dream well is what they call happiness. For there is no happiness, but only dream. What do you dream, Hulder? What is your nightmare?"

"Fiodor Kyrilovitch!" cried the American, frightened, for beads of sweat flecked the young man's brow. But Fiodor did not seem to hear. In a high, angry voice, he spoke to himself.

"Ah, you dare not reply; you're only the underman, little grovelling creature tied up by views. You believe in a God, nationality, the drawing-room; you know what is right and wrong! Fool, fool, all convictions are prisons! You say you know life is real: that of itself makes it unreal. For, man, you're dying—don't you see, dying as I speak. Can't you sniff the scent of death in every birth? That is the anodyne, the only one, the certainty of death, the only certainty . . ."

He paused, and Hulder could see that his body shook with excitement.

"Fiodor Kyrilovitch," he said gently, laying his hand upon the young man's arm, "do not speak like that. It's absurd. You're too young."

"Young!" cried Fiodor. "I, a second of space, young! Hulder, I'm only a passing mood of the life force, a puff of the great wind. A million years ago I was alive: minus a million years old, that was my age. Oh, we're old, you and I, travelling to here from so far a star, and we're dying on to an unconscious life!"

"To an unconscious life! " repeated Hulder. "Yes, that's true. We shall be, and we shall not know."

"But," screamed Fiodor, with tortured face, "how can you bear it? How can you? To die to rot, yes, I'll suffer that; but to be blotted out, not to know—I can't."

"Can you not hope? " murmured the American.

Fiodor shook his head.

"Not often. Sometimes, when I know what I am, the little atom which will join with other atoms to make the overman, I am content. Oh, some must die, those who serve and fail, the common men, the servants and the drones; but we, who feel, strive, lust, achieve, we must live, for we are life. We are the essence, we the aristocrats, we are God. And yet, in other minutes, I know that my body must go, that I cannot hope to outlive it. And soon we must face it, you and I."

"Perhaps not soon," said Hulder.

"Ha, ha," laughed Fiodor, "140, ha, ha! What fun! Schopenhauer says it would make us angry to see a day slipping away unless we were assured of eternity. Oh, what rot! What rot! And Nietzsche's secret of a good life being that we should live dangerously! We do, don't we, with death in our train? Argument and precept, falling like arrows shot at a stone wall . . ."

For a moment Hulder was terrified, for Fiodor's incoherence suggested mania, and he shook with merriment as he raved. Suddenly the Russian became serious.

"Do you read Fichte?"

"No."

"Anglais!" said Fiodor contemptuously. But his face changed; he listened.

Below them in the wood they heard a call: "Fedia! Fedia!"

"I'm here, Olia!" cried Fiodor, and as he stood up remarked: "She mustn't find me sitting on the ground." He smiled; he had shed his anger and his irony, was suddenly a mischievous child.

Slowly Olga came up the slope. As she threaded through the trees, a short, strong figure in white, a new interest awakened in Hulder. For, her white face sun-gilt and a transient flush upon her cheeks, she came supple as a hamadryad escaped from the prisoning tree. And she smiled. As she drew nearer, hidden, then visible, then half veiled by close-growing trunks, more definite, then elusive, she was a creature of the forest, one of those silent things for whom speaks the soughing night wind. As she held up a thermos flask, Hulder knew that his smile was stupid, his heart a-beating.

"Fedichka," she said, "you forgot. Your milk."

"Oh, no more milk," said Fiodor pettishly. "I hate milk."

"You must drink it," replied Olga soberly, as she unscrewed the cap and poured out the milk that was hot and steaming. "Come." She held up the cup.

"No," said Fiodor obstinately.

"Drink," she murmured. She raised the cup to Fiodor's lips, and an ache of delight went through Hulder: her brother stood upon a little mound; she had to raise her arms, and, in the white blouse, her body was close-moulded and the sun made radiant the curves of her deep bosom, while her teeth shone in the full smile of her pale face, pitifully tender, passionately adoring.

"Oh, women . . ." moaned Fiodor. Then, with a humorous smile, he drank.

"Again," she whispered. Obediently he drank once more. He wiped the white froth from his lips and said—

"Tyrant. Like all women. Don't you think so, Hulder?"

"I don't mind a woman's tyranny," said the American; "it is a gentle yoke."

He looked at Olga, thrilling a little at the soft intentness of her eyes.

"A gentle yoke?" said Fiodor more acidly. "No yoke is gentle. Shrouded in velvet, it is still a yoke."

"There I have you, Fiodor Kyrilovitch. If it is velvety you don't know it's a yoke and it ceases to be a yoke. Your own theory."

Fiodor frowned. What was this strange tightening of Olga's mouth? But he smiled, he laughed, confessed his defeat: whence came the soft curving of Olga's lips?

"True," said Fiodor; "you have scored, Hulder. But that doesn't show you're right. It only shows I'm inconsistent: and none but a fool is always consistent. You know I'm right, at the bottom; only you're an American, therefore a sentimentalist."

Hulder protested, Fiodor interrupting, Olga listening seriously. At last only did Hulder manage to state his view.

"Yes, I know what you think. You think we Americans are so busy making money that when we do see our wives, between office hours, they seem wonderful and we make fools of ourselves over them. We do, sometimes, but there's something else, Fiodor Kyrilovitch: an idea that woman is the representative of nature, the fount of the race, while man is only her defender and her helper."

"One man can keep thirty women in a harem," scoffed Fiodor.

"Yes—and we need only one man, but thirty women. We need women more, and that is why we prize them higher. Even their weakness is a claim."

For a moment, as Hulder found Olga's eyes intent upon him, he felt that a link was forging, that this attitude of mind, new to a Slav, drew her to him. But at once Fiodor burst out laughing.

"Weakness! The twentieth century and talk of woman's weakness! Good God, read a little biology, and you'll find that woman is stronger than man, only her strength has been in abeyance. And now she's trying to come to the top again, to smother us in sentimentality, to suck our blood while we sleep, to enslave us by desire into serving her. Harems! Yes, that might save us yet bars and padlocks and armed guards. Oh, not guards against other men, but guards to prevent women from harming us, drugging, deceiving us. Woman should be bought and sold. And when she has played her part as a mother, let her do the field work and all the other work of the world."

"And we men?"

"No work for us. Work's for woman; that's all she's good for."

"But," said Hulder, acid, though Fiodor shook with excitement, "if we do no work we shall decay, and then women will certainly win."

"No! Let men have learning, women their ignorance. We can hold them then as we, the aristocrats, hold the fool masses of the people. And let us keep the arms—keep the arms," he shouted; "ride, hunt, shoot, fight, and fear none."

Hulder started back, for Fiodor's face was inflamed, and yet he thought the Russian ridiculous in his rage, in his mouthings so ill-suited to his weakness, his racked body.

"Fedia!" cried Olga fearfully.

"He's a fool," growled Fiodor. A sudden change came over Olga's face.

"How dare you excite him?" the girl cried. Her cheeks became brick-red.

Fiodor stamped. "Why don't you hold your tongue?" he screamed.

"Fedia! Fedia!" Olga shouted. Then to Hulder, "You don't know what you're talking about."

Hulder stood amazed as the two turned upon him: Olga heated, hoarse with fury, stigmatizing him for an idiot, a liar; Fiodor tearful and spitting insults. Then, quite suddenly, there was silence. Fiodor drew a hand over his wet forehead.

"What have I said?" he muttered. Then, in a low voice, "I have been rude. Unjust. Oh, I am hateful! Forgive me!"

He flung himself on his knees, seized Hulder's hand. "Oh, don't hate me, don't hate me," he groaned. "Only a hundred and forty—" The American was for a moment paralyzed, for Fiodor was kissing his hand, and now Olga, too, had thrown herself at his feet: he felt her hot lips upon his hand.

"Get up, both of you," he shouted. This was too great a madness. He drew them to their feet. "Get up; of course I forgive you."

The Russians stood before him, trembling, wet-eyed. Simultaneously they each took one of Hulder's arms, began to walk with him towards the road. Then Olga said—

"Let me give you a little milk. Oh, do let me give you a little milk."

"No, thanks," said Hulder stiffly. Then, understanding her impulse, he added, "I'm not thirsty," and softly pressed her arm against his body.

"I wish you'd have a little milk," said Fiodor. "He won't," said Olga sorrowfully. "I'm afraid he won't."

Chapter V

Too great a madness? No, not yet. For two days, inevitable reaction from an intimacy too rich in incident, Hulder held a little aloof from the Russians, contented himself with nodding as he passed Fiodor, who sat reading in the sun; and he checked his desire to speak to Olga, though the grey eyes signed to him, reproachful and appealing. He struck up acquaintance with the two touristic young men, accompanied them to Starnois, where there was a dangerous rock to climb; as he talked with them of the scenery, of the respective merits of French and German wine and answered endless questions as to salaries and conditions in America, he had to own to himself that he was bored, missed the fierce stimulus of Fiodor's speeches. He was obstinate, however. Bent on giving the Russians a lesson, he went to Geneva for the day, there to yawn before the pictures in the museum, to scoff at the cheap impressionism of the Ecole Libre, and to wander silent and friendless, so long that in the end he re-entered with pleasure the train that took him to Ammenzell. Yes, he was bored; and when, later in the evening, Madame Pettinger became arch, suggested that she knew why a single gentleman went to Geneva, while the honeymoon couple giggled and the young girl in the print dress fixed upon Hulder wide, intelligent eyes, he felt incomprehensibly irritated by the cheapness of these people. He had seen, felt too much in a week to tolerate fools.

And so he was glad when, the next morning, Fiodor drew near, head a little bent and of manner gentle, to ask whether he would come for a sail with him and his sister. It was warm, though a steady breeze blew from the west; opposite the Hotel de Paris a little crowd wrangled and bargained for the sliders and the family boats; grandmothers were lowered into the capacious sterns, and from the station platform a long line of tourists passed over the bridge to the pier, where waited the steamer that was to make the round trip through Possentour and Holle. The sun hung high. As Hulder laid his hand upon a brass fitting of the boat, he exclaimed, for it burned him. And the Russians laughed, all the unease gone. As the boatman, high-seated on the stern, steered the little craft through the traffic, past the baths where the timid were noisily plunging in the shallow water, Hulder felt a great relief. The motion of the sailing boat, as it hugged the wind, smooth and deceptively swift, its veerings, light as those of a bird, as it tacked, under his eyes the flying green water that broke into strings of flashing emeralds at the bows, and the rising shore where clustered Alstanches round its modern castle, here indeed were beauty and peace. Olga sat by his side, Fiodor in the bows. They were silent, for soon they had left far behind the busy front of Ammenzell, saw it only as a row of little pink and white splotches; the boatman, seeking wind, had steered for the centre of the lake, and about them spread in heavy silence the dark green water that murmured only when some tiny wave broke against the side.

"It is beautiful," said Hulder.

There was a long pause. Then Fiodor murmured—

"La, tout n'est qu'ordre et beaute',
Luxe, calme et volupte."

And again there was silence. Indeed, for three hours, they hardly spoke at all. It was not only that they were watchful of the endless succession of woods growing close to the sedge-lined banks, of tree-crowned rocks and ruins garlanded with ivy; some unity had come to them, a unity based on Fiodor. For Olga's eyes often turned to him, and without a word she would readjust upon his shoulders the falling cape; and Hulder mingled with the blue and green vision of sky and water the picture of her firm, broad neck, her long hands, so white and blushing coral at the tips. Hungrily, he filled of her beauty, and was surprised to find in himself no jealousy, the male jealousy that cannot bear the fondness of woman when given to another. As the lovely lips smiled upon Fiodor he felt no pang, perhaps because, often, the grey eyes turned humid towards him and engaged him in some complicity to protect the brilliant weakling who joined them. "You and I," said the eyes, "we must please him. We must be patient, you and I, you know." It was wonderfully intimate and thrilling to him, absurdly grateful and sacred, so much that it brought its own reaction, that he looked away, tried to wonder what industry fed that factory upon the hill, called himself a sentimental American.

Hulder was not sentimental. He was of that quiet, calm breed that has little use for exuberant emotion. Cool, logical and a little hard, he was preoccupied with his own life, was not very much more than most men the axis of his world, but more consciously so.

Clear-eyed, he looked for happiness. He had loved, once and unfortunately, then in a looser spirit, here and there as chance would have it, in American and European cities; but buried deep in him was the conviction that the woman would yet come who would call from him something noble and thus make him noble. He looked at Olga's soft eyes, wondered and was afraid.

But the three shook off their languor and their tension. The lunch at Holle, at a little table under flowering horse-chestnut trees, was light and gay. Fiodor challenged Hulder to a drinking duel and was restrained with difficulty by Olga, who now laughed and even told one of those comic Jew stories that always delight a Russian audience. They ate too much; Hulder confided a little of his early struggles to avoid work in the United States; Fiodor became reminiscent of days at Moscow University and ended by boasting what a great man he was, while Olga indulgently laid upon his friend the soft, slow smile that meant "You and I." And, in the afternoon, in the moist grass of the meadows, they found a few white and purple flowerets that were like wild hyacinths.

But, when again they entered the boat, something in the air had changed. Suddenly the heat had fallen, and Olga anxiously swathed Fiodor's neck in the comforter. The boat scudded before the freshening wind; the boatman was more intent, for the air was fitful; continually they passed through pockets when they made hardly any headway, emerged into zones where, for a moment, the sail flapped wildly as the broken wing of a wounded bird. And, at intervals, struck by a squall, the boat heeled over, lay to the water, the gunwale flush with the hissing lines of shimmering foam. As the twilight darkened, caps of grey cloud formed upon the hills. Olga had come close to her brother, thrown one arm about his shoulders; she was calm, calmer than Hulder, who disliked the strained sound of the rigging, the fierce dips of the sail towards the brilliant little points of the waves, purplish in the sunset. But Fiodor was not calm: his eyes shone; he muttered.

"Black waves," he said, "mirrors of the night before it dawns—"

"Hush, Fedia, hush."

"Why should I? Earth or water, it's all the same. Equally they bury men. Yes," he cried, as if an intoxication seized him, "sooner or later they take us, as they will take me."

Swiftly he tore from Olga's arm. He was on his feet, clinging to the mast, despite the boatman's warning cry.

"Sooner or later!" screamed Fiodor. "What does it matter—137 or less?"

Olga, too, cried out as the boat heeled over, but already Hulder had clutched at the Russian, dragged him down; and now he held him in his arms. For a moment a glint of rage had come into Olga's eyes, but she grew soft as she listened. Hulder murmured to Fiodor, gentle, almost crooning—

"Don't be afraid, Fiodor Kyrilovitch; the water will not take you. See, I'm holding you. Feel how warm I am! Could anything harm you now?"

The Russian's eyes lost their wildness. His features relaxed

"Oh," he whispered, 'this is good." Soon he was lying passive in the sheltering arms, his head pillowed on his friend's broad breast.

Swiftly on sped the grey and mauve streamers of twilight, shade eating at the whiteness, and gold upon the hilltops to purple dying. Hulder, the thin form in his arms, conscious only of motion, had forgotten Olga. But, as the lights of Ammenzell twinkled in the night, something was impulsively thrust into his hand; it was another hand. The long, slim ringers closed round his in an intimate clasp that joined the two cold palms. He turned. In the darkness he saw Olga's eyes bathed in a soft radiance.

Chapter VI

Hulder knew that he loved. Again, inconceivably, absurdly, because a waiter had told him that he would like Ammenzell, because he had been too aimless to differ, because two Russians, one of them stricken in body, had travelled a thousand miles to a second-rate hotel on an obscure hill—preposterous that by chance the woman should come. Was love a sort of roulette? Would his heart have remained empty for ever if he had chosen the Hotel de Paris? Perhaps, unless the love passion be truly blind and the same day (who knows?) other eyes had opened. But, absurd or not, Hulder loved Olga, and all the more because, illogically, love thrives best in an atmosphere of paradox.

He knew that he loved her when she thrust her hand into his, when the thrill of the contact ran up his arm, transmuted the iciness of the clasp into a blood rush all incendiary in quality. He had said nothing, but held the hand, ground it savagely, felt a ring under his fingers and fiercely, cruelly pressed it into the cold flesh. As he looked at Olga he knew that he hated her, wished to destroy her aye, to sacrifice her, body and soul, as a burnt offering to his love of her. For the sex conflict was on him, thawing his snows. He had to make war now, to conquer; without this there could be no joyful peace. Olga had not resisted; indeed, she had returned the clasp as if begging him to hurt her, to set his imprint upon her—to connect her in a wild trinity of passion with the boy whom he held fast against his breast.

But it was love, too, this cruelty. Hulder had stood face to face with her at the gates, the lights streaming upon his comeliness, his small head, his short-cropped, curly hair; he seemed to her so steadily blue-eyed, so square-chinned, big and reliant as a rock. For a moment she had wondered whether he could help her. She had wanted to cry out—

"Oh, save him, save him! He is my brother, myself, my love. Dispel his wildness, restore his body, give him strength—and I am yours, your lover, your servant, your squaw, to toy with or beat or kill."

But Olga had held herself in too many years, too much schooled herself into calmness so that Fiodor might be soothed. All that she could do was to look up at Hulder humbly, tell him who they were.

"We are twins," she said. "Our parents are dead, and Fiodor was studying law at Moscow. But—one lung was touched; we went to Crimea where there are vines. It was no good—one lung was destroyed—we travelled everywhere: Davos, the Italian coast, Algiers; everywhere it was too high or too low, or too hot—the sweats of night—oh, my God, oh, my God! " She hid her face in her hands. Then, more assured;

"So we came here; the doctors said that this was not too high, but sometimes—"

"Sometimes?" asked Hulder gently, drawing her hands down.

"The other lung, too." Her face was now livid. "Sometimes I think—"

"Oh, Olga!" Hulder, still holding her hands, drew her towards him. She did not resist, for now she talked feverishly. Her self-control gone, she told everything. They were free, they had money, but she feared Fiodor was dying. And worse, he knew. Some doctor, some brute, some fool, in Lucerne she thought, had given way to him, told him he had only six months to live. He counted the days one by one.

"Ah!" cried Hulder, understanding at last. "That's why he said 137—137 days."

"Let me go! " snarled the girl. As she tore herself out of his grasp Hulder saw the mask of a fury, and shrank away.

But, next day, she came soft, as if she had given herself by giving her confidence. Stronger indeed was her faith, for that day again it was the will of the American saved Fiodor from ending his dance of death. It was he thrust away the young man, snatched from his hands the steering-wheel of the motor-car into which he had beguiled them. All had gone well, but at the top of Starnois hill Fiodor had suddenly put on speed, and with a cry of "135" headed straight for the down grade. While Olga sat limp at the back of the car, she had watched as a prey for which wild beasts fight the struggle for the wheel—heard the quiet, hurried "Let go, Fiodor," of the American, the horrible, steady proclamation of her brother's numbered days. She had sat, hands gripping the sides, while the car miraculously swayed through a curve felt herself rocking seen a white wall towards which she seemed to travel swift as a flying spear— and then her brother had been struck in the face before her eyes—she had fainted.

She sat up upon the grass. The two men knelt trembling by her side.

"Fedia!" she cried; drew him down, kissed his cheek. Then her face set. "You!" she said savagely to Hulder. " You struck him I You dared—"

"To save him."

"Oh!" She staggered to her feet. "Oh, I am mad! You struck him—I hate you, loathe you. No, you saved him. I owe you his life. Oh, forgive me."

She flung herself at Hulder's feet. He laid a hand upon her shoulder. She shrank away. "How dare you touch me with your murdering hand?"

And again, in constant alternation of feeling, she had come to him. With every mood of her brother she had changed in her attitude to the American, as if some mysterious correspondence of feeling were established between them. It was an uncertain, dangerous companionship, and Hulder wondered why he tolerated it, why he bore with what he now believed to be madness in the young man; though he wondered, he knew; only he would not acknowledge the truth too readily. This mother passion in Olga had stimulated in him something more profound than the ever fiercer attraction of her; as she stood or walked by his side a desire began to gnaw at him, until he had to knot his hands together for fear he should publicly seize her, bend back the white pillar of her neck and crush under his the pouting, purplish mouth, but he knew that a streak, all mental that one, pierced through and coloured the fury of sense. He wanted her love, and the tenderness of her, to have her lightest caress, to have her for sister, companion, friend as well as lover.

For she was as a broad river flowing slowly between low banks. And even when in spate she had her majesty.

Fiodor, humble and for a while conquered, as if he were a woman, as if male strength had daunted him and made him joyous, had walked the road with Hulder, his arm about his neck. Soon Olga had come to them, and the moon had shed upon them a pale green radiance. She had allowed Hulder to take her arm; then, unrebuked, to slide his hand along her forearm, hold her hand, under cover of the night to play, one by one, half purposeful, half sportive, with the long, lax fingers she yielded him. Hulder stood linked to two parallel emotions, as if in the grip of some composite force that acted and reacted through two elements. He was as a cork floating in a bowl of water that communicated with another; if water were poured into the first bowl he rose in the second. And for him there were no local storms. One night, when a discussion of the Slav temperament involved him, when he praised Dostoievsky, only to be told that this literary bungler tried to drive a three-horse chariot, but harnessed one of his steeds to the tail, when once more Fiodor was contemptuous and angry, Olga snatched away her hand.

And yet, next morning, Fiodor wept in his bed, prayed that his American friend might bring him his breakfast and talk to him. Then Olga came, half commanding and half entreating. Without challenge she laid both hands upon the American's arm.

"I can't go on," thought Hulder; "I don't know what I'm doing."

Indeed, he hardly knew how to hold those two. He had not before known love and friendship as hair shirts, nor had he known them to rush as dragons across his path. At school, at college and in later years, friendship had slowly blossomed for him; acquaintance had warmed into something closer; then confidence had been given and reciprocated; dreams and hopes had shyly come out of concealment, and then, sometimes, intimacy had arisen, a community of feeling and desire; but never before, in less than a fortnight, had he found himself forced into a close relation with strangers, a relation emotional on the one side and on the other passionate. Everything that he felt was contrary to American practice and to American tradition, for neither Olga nor Fiodor had eluded him; the young man had revealed himself at once as fierce, half desperate and certainly hysterical. He had allowed, his new friend to understand his distresses, and Hulder knew that Fiodor knew that he knew the secret of his malady. Himself thoughtful and intuitive, he was capable of grasping something of the tumultuous emotions which racked Fiodor's decaying body and threatened to shake it to pieces as over-powerful machinery slowly loosens the plates of a small ship. He guessed very well the origin of the ferocity with which Fiodor viewed his fellows; it was not surprising that the beauty of sky, flower, woman and beast should arouse in the heart of the young Russian, together with a powerful aesthetic delight, an unbearable hatred.

Hulder was not surprised when, quite suddenly, Fiodor told him that he hated the world because it would survive him, that he hated lovers because they would still love when he was rotting, that he hated beauty, and joy, and gaiety, because these things were eternal, and that if he believed in any God he would pray to Him to let him live so long that about him, as the sun slowly lost its heat and the internal fire of the earth died, he might see the ice gaining upon the land, the flowers wither, the fog obscure the sun until it was no more than a poor yellowish disc which he might outstare. He wished to see man become again what man had been when he emerged from the ape: a creature without intellect, dominated by nothing save its passions, incapable of feeling love, ambition or hope, capable only of understanding those things that the beasts understand: fear, lust, hunger and cold, until at last he might see man crouching, naked and hideous, in a stone cave, and his mate no longer scented, playing Puccini, and dressing in Paris, but now no more than the brute with long hair whom her master might beat or kill. At last, he might, as the cold gripped closer the ball of the earth, assist at the death agony of the last man. And then in the desert, when the earth was dead and no more in space than another moon, he would gladly give up life, for he would have been the last of mankind, the greatest of the aristocrats.

Yes, he understood. For indeed it is not easy to conceive the earth without oneself. None can fill the gap left by one's disappearance. One does not disappear—one changes; and belief in God and survival is, after all, only a certainty that one carries within oneself a spark of defined essence, which means that one will not merge into the Godhead: no, more arrogantly, man hopes to merge God Himself into his own immense and terribly vivid personality. Belief in the future life is blasphemy in disguise. It was not wonderful, thought Hulder, that a dying man, such as Fiodor, should blaspheme: who, more than a dying man, had a right to curse earthly life?

It was not, however, upon Fiodor that most of Hulder's thoughts dwelt. Little by little, as by a tide that slowly rose, obliterating the foreshore, he had been absorbed by Olga's personality. At first mysterious, hardly comprehensible, it had struck him merely as self-centred, expectant and brooding; he had thought that she lacked vitality, merely existed as some beautiful flower of the field. But he had changed his metaphor, begun to realize her more as a spreading tree under which a man could shelter from the sun. He had discovered her as a creature with a single passion, as twin of body to her brother, also twin of soul. All that was in Fiodor she, too, contained: his fierceness, his love of the beautiful, his sweetness, all the intolerable conflict of spirit and sense that made him up. But these currents of her ran under a placid surface: she was potential where her brother was actual. Those furies when Fiodor was displeased with him, they were Fiodor's furies at one remove, and her smiles were smiled by Fiodor through her mouth. On the day when Hulder knew that he loved her he was indeed disturbed by a new sense: if she was Fiodor in woman's form, through her he loved Fiodor or both of them; and he loved them inextricably as if he had conceived a comic, a tragic passion for the Siamese twins. It was ridiculous, and yet it was wonderful, for that day, when for the first time he held Olga's hand, he could hardly divest himself of the feeling that some maleness had crept into the girl's features; he almost expected to see falling over her left eye an untidy mass of black hair.

Fiodor wished, that afternoon, to be alone, so they had left him sitting upon a bench on a hillock, reading an unexciting English novel, his cape wrapped about him and the red and green comforter so closely wound about his neck that all that could be seen of him was a rather pinched yellow nose and two brilliant eyes. He looked, more than ever, like an anxious and excited crow. He had promised to go home as soon as the sun went down, and now together, in the heat of the day, Hulder and Olga walked away, passing the garden of warring clematis, towards the lake. When they reached the banks and saw the water shining dully like molten lead under a haze of heat, Olga clasped her hands together, bent her head. In that moment she was all languor, and Hulder wondered where, when far from her brother, all that energy which she devoted to the maintaining of his life lay dormant. He did not, however, very long watch the play of the wind on her black hair; he was too active in mind to remain thus quiescent.

"Shall we take a boat?" he asked.

"If you like," said Olga.

Slowly he pulled out toward the middle of the lake. Olga, half sitting, half lying against the cushions, seemed abandoned and lax as Hulder sculled almost unaware of the rhythmic movement of his body. He wondered what thoughts coursed under that low white brow, and he was stung into desiring those thoughts should be thoughts of him, for she was very beautiful as she thus lay. The sun, striking beyond the brim of her straw hat, had found gaps between the black strands of hair that fell low upon her forehead, and patterned her features with a queer criss-cross of dark lines that threw into relief the dead whiteness of her skin. Eyes closed, eyelashes making shadows upon the high cheeks, mouth a little open as if in some momentary weakness appealing for strength, long hands, lax and languid as bending sprays of fern. And joined with this weakness, this woman softness of her, was the incongruous woman's strength of her broad shoulders, of the strong curves of her breast, deep flanks and slim hard-knit limbs under her flimsy skirt. She was beautiful, intolerably: as a woman, fierce bearer of passion, and yet sweet, weak toy, hard-handled by another's pain.

As he pulled, Hulder wanted to tell her that he loved her, for he had not done so yet though he had touched her and though her lips had been upon his hand. He wanted slowly to ship the sculls, to kneel, to throw himself by her side, draw her hands to his cheeks and, his face hidden on her breast, to murmur the avowal of his passion. Yet he was so surrounded, so saturated by the atmosphere of the common curse they bore, that when at last they spoke, it was this he said—

"I wonder what Fiodor is doing?"

There was a silence and then, suddenly, Olga said—

"Do not let us talk about Fiodor."

Very slowly the significance of this stirred the American, and, with a beating heart, he slowly turned the bows of the boat towards the shore where, near Alstanches, the trees came down to the water to drink. Olga had opened her eyes, and now, grey and immense, they stared into the sky above Hulder's head, stealing from the heavens a little of their purple radiance. They did not speak, either of them, as silently and swiftly Hulder urged the boat towards the shore. Soon they slid within the shelter of the willows that hung about them their tender green curtain, their drooping twigs. The willows stooped, firm-planted in the earth, towards the water, here and there caressing it with twig or leaf, as if tree and water were wedding. Soundlessly, as a swan moving stately upon a pond, the boat passed under the interminable arch that the trees made as they succeeded one another along the line of the shore; slower and slower came the strokes of the sculls, and closer and closer was the air about them as grew the sense of solitude and of the unity of two. Hulder found that his strokes were losing their power, his arms moving more slowly until, by almost imperceptible degrees, the boat stopped before the wall of giant bulrushes that grew across the water in steep plantation.

Careless of the sculls which floated on the dead water, Hulder slid from his seat. Again his heart was beating and some keen disappointment worked in him because still Olga seemed unaware of him. She seemed so aloof, so remote from him, that his uncertain purpose again wavered, that he felt tempted so to remain in the cool shadow of the branches, to fill his eyes with all this beauty about him, and with that to be content. The beating of his heart accorded ill with the languor that was upon him, a languor that with every second seemed to gain upon him, to press down his limbs with soft, velvety but leaden hands. He wished that this state might last for ever, wondered a little whether it had always been. And yet there was anxiety in him.

Suddenly Olga looked up, fixed her eyes upon his. She did not speak or smile, but there was a softness in her look which Hulder did not analyze because he did not mistake it. Almost unconsciously he bent forward, slowly slid from his seat towards the girl and then, without intent, he was by her side, out stretched, and he had taken Olga's hand, drawn her arm round his neck. His head resting against her, he softly drew her hand to his cheek and then, very softly, pressed his lips into the warm palm. Olga did not resist, nor was there in the contact of her hand any sign that she felt or desired the caress. Her eyes were closed now, and for a very long time those two stayed, very close and linked, conscious of their nearness to each other, and yet perhaps of something unsaid, that must by and by be said, that would more truly link them. As they lay, side by side, Hulder knew himself invaded by a content he had never before known, as if this girl were by her quiescence, by the calm protectiveness of her, giving him that rest and security which he had never found in the common turbulence of passion. He was conscious less of her than of the fact of her, as he might have been conscious of the purple vault which he could glimpse through the branches of the trees. With her arm about him, inactive but strong, he was as a child at its mother's breast.

They had lost the sense of time, and time fleeted. It was Olga first knew that something of the oppressiveness of the heat had gone, guessed that upon the dull waters the shadows were lengthening.

"We must go," she murmured.

Hulder, still in his dream, did not reply. Suddenly, a closer sense of life filled him, for Olga's fingers had acquired some new and purposeful energy. He felt them move upon his cheek, softly caressing. They dwelt about the strong hard line of his shaven chin; with smooth, firm tips they pressed into his cheek. And, at last, it was the whole of Olga's hand that had drawn his head closer to her, so close that against his ear he could feel the steady beating of her heart. Within him an activity seemed to quicken. Seizing her hand, he turned and very close looked into eyes that met his, grave and tender. His mouth moved, he wanted to speak and could not, for too much was rushing out of his most intimate being, too great was his desire to tell her he wanted her, needed her, was her master and her slave, would be her conquest and her conqueror.

He held her in his arms and, though they did not speak, they knew, both of them, that they needed little more besides this etheric communication. Even his hunger for her lips had vanished in Hulder's dumb, passionate desire for self-expression. He wanted her now more than her lips. Olga understood. Without pushing him away, she sat up in her seat, still looking into his eyes, then very gravely—

"We must go."

Without a word Hulder released her, and as he did so she gave him a long, slow smile, a smile more confident and linking, because a smile accomplice, than would have been a caress.

Again began the rhythmic swing of the sculls. Full-stretched upon the cushions as the sun went down, Olga was bathed in the dying brightness of its gold.

But once they reached land and the charm was broken by a brief quarter of an hour under the little red and white umbrellas of the floating tea place, Olga was no longer merry, no longer insisted upon feeding with cake the numerous dogs which went begging about the tables. She changed. Something urgent began to pervade her manner, as if the life that an hour before had been so remote, when she lay under the willows, had seized her again and was again beginning to dominate her. She was anxious.

"We must hurry," she said. "We have been away too long. I wonder what Fedia has been doing? Perhaps"—and a note of fear was in her voice—"perhaps he has not gone back to the hotel when the sun went down."

She started up and Hulder had to pull her down to her seat.

"Oh," she cried, "he's so imprudent. We must go. We must go."

And all along the road she was silent and hurried. Hulder had to stretch to their utmost his long limbs to keep pace with her swift, nervous paces; upon the flat she ran heedless of his protests and assurances that doubtless all was well with her brother. And she was breathless when, at length, she leapt up the steps of the National, ran up the stairs. Hulder followed, and laughed aloud as Fiodor met them upon the first landing, book in hand, quite calm, smiling, wearing not only the cape but even the comforter. But he was charmed as he saw the change upon Olga's face. Hardness and anxiety had gone. She blushed faintly in her delight as if, in her mother soul, day had dawned.

"Come upstairs into my room," said Fiodor. "There's an hour before dinner. I have talked to nobody to-day, and that's bad for me, isn't it, Olichka?"

"You talk too much," said Olga, with mock severity. "That's why you talk such nonsense."

"Nonsense or not," said Fiodor good-humouredly, "I must talk. I'll let any doctor have my life," he added grimly, "but not my tongue. Come along, Hulder."

The American followed him into his room, and at once Fiodor began to talk as if indeed three hours of silence had been more than his restless spirit could bear.

"Do you know," he said excitedly, "last night I had a dream! A terrible, a wonderful dream! Listen." He whispered, very quickly, " I wanted to tell you this morning and then changed my mind. Listen: three elephants came slowly, one behind the other, and each had a wreath of peonies upon his head, and behind were more elephants, and yet more elephants. I couldn't see them, and I knew they were there—and upon the first elephant rode the figure of Death, upon the second elephant an angel with your face, upon the third elephant was Madame Pettinger." He laughed. "Wasn't it funny because, among all the elephants I couldn't see, I knew there were baby elephants."

"Madame Pettinger's baby elephants," said Hulder, laughing.

"Perhaps," said Fiodor seriously, as if he had not meant his "Wasn't it funny?"

"Listen; it isn't finished. The three elephants began to trumpet all together, and I could understand. They were calling to the invisible elephants behind, and this is what they were calling: ' Elephants, old elephants, young elephants, where are you, O elephants?' And then, from very far away, came a faint trumpeting: 'We are dead, and we are unborn. It is all the same.' Then an organ-grinder began to grind and the elephants began to dance, and I heard Madame Pettinger say, 'Hurry, Maria, with the coffee.' But it wasn't Madame Pettinger calling; it was another elephant, a very little white one, and, as soon as the word 'coffee' was spoken, that one, too, began to trumpet and to cry out: 'Where are you, O elephants, old elephants, young elephants?'

"And then, very far away, came the low trumpeting as they answered: 'We are in the National eating sausage.' But I knew it wasn't true—and yet I believed it—because I seemed to know that there was nothing true. . . . What are you laughing at?"

Hulder had thrown himself back in his chair, and was laughing aloud. It was not only that the dream struck him as absurd; he, too, had had these curious dreams where the material mingled with the fantastic, but Fiodor's tragic seriousness struck him as irresistibly funny.

"What is there to laugh at?" Nazimov repeated. "It isn't funny; it's significant."

"Are you going to read your future from dreams, Fedia?" said Hulder.

"My future? " said Nazimov contemptuously. "Of course not. The future needs no reading; the future is death. Dreams tell us something, don't you know?"

"Yes, they tell us something about indigestion."

"Tush," cried Fiodor. "How can you talk like that? You don't dream when you are awake, even if you have got indigestion. It's your other self speaking, your foreconscious self."

"Foreconscious?" said Hulder, puzzled.

"Yes, the foreconscious self in the subliminal plane. Don't you understand? Have you never heard of Freud—of psycho-analysis—of Jung of Zurich?"

Hulder looked at him, blankly, but Fiodor had forgotten him and was expounding at length the Freud method. He was so excited, he spoke so fast, that Hulder could gather only roughly that dreams released a self, of which we were not conscious, located between our conscious self and our unconscious self. That was the foreconscious self. If we could analyze it by the method of free association between patient and operator, by questions evoking responses, we could discover early mental lesions, old, painful impressions upon the brain, to which were due our phobias, blind fears of trifles and our inhibitions, those incapacities to do or to bear.

"Yes," Fiodor cried excitedly, "the dream is the key. Thus, when we lie defenceless in the arms of night, our secret hidden soul comes forth, all seared and torn by life. Oh, I'm glad I dreamt I so seldom dream. That dream shall be read." His excitement grew. "I'll go to Freud; he shall read me. He shall make me see the things I fear." His smile became beatific. "And I shall fear no more."

"Why not?" asked Hulder.

Fiodor looked at him with gleaming eyes. "Why not? You say, 'Why not?' But then," he cried gleefully, "you understand? You believe?"

"Oh, well," said Hulder. "Why not try?"

Fiodor's expression became sour. "Oh," he said, "empiricism, that's all." Then, after a pause. "Anglais!"

Hulder laughed. He was amused when Fiodor, looking for the most stinging insult he could think of, called him an Englishman. But Fiodor did not mind. Even half-agreement was enough to satisfy him. Already he smiled again.

"Oh, yes, you've your doubts, and no wonder. One always has one's doubts before one knows; but you're not afraid, are you? You're American; you like the new. Oh, you are a wonderful people, accepting, open-eyed, the good and the bad." His excitement grew. "And you, Hulder, you're wonderful, so calm, so resolute, and you always know what I mean, though I know it's difficult. It's my fault; I am difficult. Perhaps I'm mad sometimes, and there you are, always ready, always indulgent. You know what I mean. You do, you do," he cried. "You're the only one who has ever known."

"I tried," said Hulder.

Fiodor seized his hand. "Yes, I know." Then, very seriously, "I did not think there could be elective affinities between men, but there is one between you and me, is there not?"

"Yes," said Hulder gravely, and, as he spoke, thought of Olga.

"Elective affinity," Nazimov repeated. "Hulder, we have a common ego, you and I." His grasp tightened. "Will you be my blood-brother?"

"Of course I will, Fedia," said Hulder.

Nazimov gave a little cry of delight, and at once Hulder found himself a party to an extraordinary scene. Nazimov took a glass from the washstand, rilled it with water. Then, opening a penknife and pushing up to the elbow the sleeve of his velvet coat, he dug the blade into his thin arm: there was a little spurt of blood which he caught in the glass of water. Then, mutely, he held out the knife to the American. Hulder hesitated. Unconsciously he recoiled. He had heard vaguely the details of this barbarous rite, and was willing enough to subject himself to it, but the knife, all bloody, was an unpleasant object. Under Fiodor's burning eyes he drew his scarf-pin, gingerly grazed his wrist, and pressed out a few drops of blood into the glass.

A cry escaped him, for Fiodor had gulped down one half of the contents, and now, with a rigid, maniacal expression upon his face, was holding out the remainder to him. Evidently he was to drink his share. At that moment a thrill of horror ran right through the American's body, for the mixture, he knew, was all animate with bacteria. To humour Fiodor, yes; to risk consumption, no; and yet he shrank from offending the young man in whom, with every second of hesitation, fury seemed to grow. But the fear was too great.

"No," he said briefly. "That is not the custom of my country. Our blood has mixed; we are blood-brothers; but I will not drink."

There was no reply, but, with a swift movement, Fiodor threw the blood-tinged water into his face, half blinding him and, in the same second, as Hulder closed with him, he heard a crash against the wall which showed that Fiodor had also thrown the glass at his head. For some seconds they wrestled silently, for Hulder had no breath to spare in restraining a strength that was all mania, while from Fiodor came only a series of low animal growls. Quite suddenly he collapsed, and Hulder threw him down on his back upon the bed. For some time Fiodor remained quiescent in his grasp, but still glowering, his spirit untamed in his weak body; then little by little his features returned to normal. The look in his eyes became soft. When at last Hulder released him his face was twisted in agony. He slid to his knees, seized the American's hands. "Forgive me," he muttered. "I'm a dog. I'm uncivilized, a barbarian. Oh, yes, yes," he cried, as Hulder tried to speak, for he was now anxious to abase himself, "I am a Hun, I am not a Westerner at all. I am a savage. You are the people of the West, the people furthest from the beasts. Oh, forgive me, forgive me."

His voice broke and there were tears in it. The sobs grew, rose up from his throat, tearing, choking little sobs which, as they increased in intensity, blended into a horrible, continuous moan.

Hulder stood paralyzed in his grasp, unable to think of anything to do or say. And, at that moment, the door opened; Olga came in. She did not look at Hulder. As if impelled by some automatic device, she ran to the kneeling figure, seized it by both shoulders, lifted it on to the bed and at once, as she bent over Fiodor, her voice was soft and crooning. She begged him to tell her what had happened, what had been done to him, and many times she pressed kisses upon his tear-stained cheeks. She rocked him in her arms until, little by little, Fiodor's moans became less loud, until at last they ceased, and he remained pale and exhausted, his head upon her breast.

In that silence Hulder spoke. "I'm very sorry," he said.

Olga looked up at him with an air of surprise as if just aware of his presence.

"Sorry!" she repeated, and her eyes lit up as if she realized his connection with Fiodor's state. "What have you been doing to him?" she snarled. "What have you said? You've insulted him! How dare you insult him? Go away, go away; I don't want to see you. Go away," she cried, louder, and the soles of her feet began to tap as if she, too, were near the hysterical line.

After a second's hesitation Hulder thought it best to obey. His knees seemed to fail him when he went, so intense and racking had been the little incident, and so wounded was he by its sequel.

The evening dragged out. Hulder thought he would leave Ammenzell, abandon these madmen, find some place where there would be peace. But he did not know where to go. Perhaps he did not want to go. And he remembered Olga's eyes, the glow in them when she was angry, almost as wonderful as their humid tenderness when she melted to him. He would go, but could not.

At eleven o'clock that night, when he was sitting on his balcony and about to go to bed, he heard in the stillness, coming through the open window, a conversation in Russian, in excited tones. He did not understand, but when at last, quite suddenly, there came pealing through the night the same set of words, maniacally screamed, he knew what was happening: it was Fiodor calling in despair the dwindling account of the days he had to live.

Chapter VII

Fiodor fell in love. He had been alone down into the town to buy cigarettes. At the shop where he usually bought them there were that day none of the brand which he affected. Still muffled in his cape, with the comforter hanging loosely about his neck, he walked quickly through the narrow streets. The sun was streaming upon him; he was warmed and gay.

He stopped before a little shop where, behind a large show of porcelain pipes, of picture postcards and photograph frames, were stacked packets of cigarettes. Across the showcase was painted in large letters the name of the owner, Treitzen. He went in. The jangling little bell brought to the counter a girl. Smiling, she bent towards him, but Fiodor did not speak. With burning, hungry eyes he analyzed every detail of her, the plaited flaxen hair, the soft blue eyes, the perfect pink and white of her cheeks and neck, and the wonder of her little teeth set in very red, rather full lips that smiled at him humbly and yet very tenderly, as if capable of expressing only the gentleness of love, almost motherly. She bent a little further forward.

"Monsieur desire?"

Fiodor did not reply, for her movement had brought out in her arms and breast gracious curves which promised the woman a beauty greater than was given the girl. Staring at her, he yearned for her, felt as if some call were issuing from his body towards hers. She was still smiling as, hoarsely, he said—

"What is your name?"

"Elise, Monsieur" she replied, and was as calm as if his question were the ordinary preliminary to a purchase.

"Elise," he repeated. "It's a beautiful name, and you are beautiful."

The girl blushed; from her forehead to the edge of her low-necked blouse she was as a rose petal. "You are beautiful," Fiodor repeated. Then, leaning a little forward, his eyes fixed upon hers, which quite frankly met his, as if too innocent to be afraid, he said, "I love you."

Elise looked away. "Mais . . . Monsieur!" she murmured. She was confused, but not displeased.

The sun had brought out some colour in Fiodor's pale cheeks; his black hair was ordered that day and, though slight of figure, he, too, was beautiful.

"I love you," Fiodor repeated, and without any hesitation he slid his hands forward, took those of the girl, who but faintly resisted him, bent across the counter, drew her towards him so that her half-averted face rested against his cheek, and kissed her upon the lips.

Chapter VIII

Fiodor was gay; Fiodor was exuberant. His conquering tread raised the dust upon the white road and, as he walked, he sang light little mazurkas, scraps of operas, and even two or three bars of the old Russian ballad, "Over the river, the soft, flowing river, bends the weeping willow."

Upon the steps of the National stood Hulder, rigid, prepared to be offended still, but Fiodor had forgotten: what was sympathy or blood brotherhood to a lover? He seized the American's hands.

"Oh, Hulder," he cried, "I'm so happy, I'm so happy. Isn't everything wonderful? See, there's a hawk in the sky." He pointed to a tiny speck hovering high above. "The hawk, he'll get his quarry soon, and—I oh, Hulder, I want to dance." He ground the American's hands in a hard clasp and then bounding up the steps of the hotel, was gone.

"Another change," thought Hulder. "Still, a welcome one." Indeed, it was a welcome change, for an hour later, when he arrived for lunch a little late, at the small table which he shared with the Nazimovs, he found a new Olga waiting for him; no longer the mouthing, fierce Olga of the previous night, but one who greeted him with a smile soft as velvet.

Fiodor did not hide his secret. There seemed no reason why he should, and if there had been he could not have resisted sharing with them his intolerable delight. Each one in turn was told the details of the adventure and other details as they came. He hid nothing, neither the impulse that had come upon him nor the way in which he had succumbed to it. It seemed to him natural that he should respond so swiftly to the girl's appeal, that he should recognize without any of the little shammings and coquetries which make up human intercourse the fact that, as he looked into Elise's eyes, a new shaping had come to his destiny.

"Isn't it just a little—sudden?" suggested Hulder.

"Sudden!" cried Fiodor. "Of course it's sudden. Isn't a thunderclap sudden? Doesn't a mushroom come up in a night? And does the crocus hesitate when it thrusts up through the soil its little white and purple sheath? "

"True enough," said Hulder. "But then you forget: the storm has piled up for a long time, while the crocus and the mushroom grow very long under the soil."

Fiodor looked at him contemptuously. "And do you really think," he said, "that love doesn't pile up and grow? Why, love amasses in every one of us for days and weeks and years. Amasses and concentrates until, almost at bursting point, it rushes forth into the open like the devil, as a roaring lion, seeking whom he may devour."

"Indeed!" said Hulder, still sceptical. "Then your love is impersonal? It burst forth and Elise happened to be there, and you're going to eat her? Good heavens, Fiodor, one hour's delay and it might have been Mrs. Pettinger your devouring lion encountered. What an escape for both of you! "

Fiodor shrugged his shoulders. "Anglais!" he said. But he was too happy to remain offended. Newly a lover, he had to persuade all men that he was a lover. More than that, he wished all men to be lovers, so that his passion might thrive in an atmosphere where all worshipped as he.

"Hulder," he said gravely, "you're only pretending not to understand. You, too, you know it. The great adventures of life are like dragons that lie in hiding by the side of the road; they rush out upon you suddenly, stand across your path and bid you fight. There's no time for delay then, and you know when your time has come." He bent upon the American eyes that seemed curiously lucid. "You, too," he repeated, "you know."

And Hulder was silent, for at that moment Olga's eyes suddenly met his and, with a shock, he realized that this was true: he, too, almost as soon as Fiodor, he had known. And he wondered whether Fiodor also knew his secret, or whether the egotism of the invalid was so great that he was unaware of anything that passed outside his immediate^ mental circle.

All that day Fiodor talked to him, wildly, without end, to Olga almost as continually, but with the note of caution which a son would adopt towards his mother, of Elise and Elise's charms. "She is like the peach, the peony, and the white of the lily chases upon her cheek the jealous colour of the rose; her hair is like a ripple on the lake when the sun gilds it; her mouth is like a bow carved in the flesh of a pomegranate . . . and shy and tender is she as a fleeting doe—as a fleeting doe anxious to be slain. And, bending, she is like a reed in the embrace of the wind . . ."

His melancholy lifted. He was intoxicated with the new wine poured into the old bottle of his life.

"She is everything I've been waiting for, the sweetness, the softness and the calm. And she is the love hunger and the sting of love. She did not resist me, for why should she? Was I not the one for whom she had waited her eighteen years, and those thousands of years during which she was in the making? I adore her; I'm drunk of her."

Indeed, he was drunk of her and, as Hulder considered him, his grey eyes darker in their wildness and his black hair matted over his left eyebrow, his little moustache trembling with the intensity of his feeling, he felt anxious, afraid of this new passion so strong in its uprush, and so daunting. It was as if Fiodor, cold in the shadow of death, had suddenly been reanimated by the promise of life, and yet, knowing this promise to be false or transient, had sworn to draw from life all he could while he could, to gather while he might the roses of lips, and all this was so wild, so strange, because the gravedigger hung so close behind the ringer of the wedding bells.

Hulder went to Olga, spoke a few of his fears.

"He is very excited," he said, when Fiodor had disappeared, evidently to walk up and down before Treitzen's windows to catch a glimpse of Elise.

"Are you surprised?" asked Olga.

"No, of course not. But still, whatever he says, it seems so extraordinary."

"Yes," said Olga gravely. "He always is extraordinary it's amazing, you see she's not even a girl of his own class."

"I don't say that matters much, but still—"

"But still," said Olga, with a rather ironic smile, "but still it does matter, and yet you don't really think it matters."

"No," said Hulder. "After all, it doesn't matter. Love, like God, has no respect of persons."

For a moment, as their eyes met, they achieved unity, and there trembled upon Hulder's lips the avowal of his own passion, for he, too, was inflamed by this atmosphere which Fiodor was creating, anxious to follow his example, but the disquiet in him was too great to allow him to express himself just then. He had another preoccupation, that of Fiodor himself, because the rigidity of an almost New England conscience made him feel responsible for what was happening.

"There is something else," he said, "that troubles me. His—his state of health."

"Well?" said Olga, rather harshly.

"I don't want to exaggerate, but still—you know what I mean."

"I don't, or rather I do. And what has that got to do with it?"

"Surely," said Hulder, "you must see what I mean. The girl doesn't know—how ill he is." He looked sideways at Olga, rather anxiously, fearing an outburst, but apparently she was taking the discussion as if it affected a general question.

"No," she said, "of course the girl doesn't know, and she mustn't."

"Mustn't?" cried Hulder. "But really it isn't quite fair."

"Fair?" said Olga vaguely, the idea of fairness evidently a little foreign to her. "I'm not talking of that. But don't you think it splendid that Fiodor should be so happy?"

"But the girl, the girl!" cried Hulder.

"Well, what of the girl? " asked Olga, quite placid. "I'm talking of Fedia."

Hulder was silent for a moment, realizing that Olga saw no side save that of Fiodor. But still he had to make another effort.

"I see what you mean," he said. "But he can't—marry her!"

"Marry her? " said Olga, surprised. "Of course he can't marry her, but why should he?"

"He—he—" faltered Hulder. "If he can't marry her, then surely it can't go on."

"Why not?"

"It'll make her so unhappy if she doesn't know; if she's in love with him—which I can hardly believe— she'll break her heart when she finds out."

"That's quite possible," said Olga coldly. But a glowing warmth came into her voice. "Don't you think it splendid that Fiodor should be so happy? "

Hulder surrendered. He knew that he had made no impression at all upon Olga's point of view, which was soft as the tenderest flesh where she loved, steel-hard towards the rest of the world. Though he had failed, he felt closer drawn towards her. A tigress, perhaps, but had she not lain very close in his arms? And would it not be wonderfully warm and heartening if it were he, the object of that passion so capable of concentrating itself upon one creature to the exclusion of all others? And yet his conscience bade him intervene between the fresh young girl and the consumptive, perhaps the madman, who threatened the safety of her body and soul.

Very shyly, that night, he spoke to Fiodor, only to be met by a mixture of blank incomprehension, as in Olga, and of rhapsodies on the perfections of the new love. He dared not, for fear of a scene and the crying of a fateful number of days, speak quite plainly. It would not have mattered much if he had, for Fiodor, intoxicated with his new delight, had forgotten death, glimpsed immortality. One little thing, though, Hulder did: remembering the scene in the boat, not many days old, he suggested to Fiodor that he had better not take the girl upon the lake, for he had a terrifying vision of Fiodor, suddenly overwhelmed by the fear of impending death, deciding to forestall its blow, and to go to it in the arms of his beloved. Artfully, he suggested to Nazimov that he was liable to catch cold upon the lake. He rallied him, told him Elise would have no use for him if he blew his nose all the time. But Fiodor laughed and replied—

"I'll catch no cold now, Hulder. I couldn't: La fortune favorise les amants. Nothing can touch me."

As he spoke there was such a glow of youth and health in his face that, for a moment, Hulder wondered whether indeed this were new life, whether Elise's love could perform a miracle denied the doctors. And then, realizing himself as helpless, he felt that events must take their course. Elise must take risks, and if she took them with closed instead of with open eyes, that could not be helped, for another sharp scene with Olga had followed upon his attempt to induce Fiodor to avoid the lake.

Olga had suspected in him a desire to step in between Fiodor and his happiness. She had come to him with that close knot in her eyebrows which Hulder knew and feared.

"How dare you interfere? " she asked. " What has it to do with you?"

Hulder once more stated his case.

"Don't be ridiculous," said Olga. "That day in the boat he was nervous, upset. It was nothing, just an accident."

"It might happen again," said Hulder gravely.

"It will not happen again; he's too happy."

"Yes," said Hulder, "he is happy." And there was little longing in his voice. Olga's next words were less harsh, but still firm.

"You must not deny Fiodor pleasure," she said. "Both of us, we must do what we can."

And Hulder felt a little shame because so many of his scruples vanished when this woman, whom he feared and loved, said "both of us." It was ignominious, he knew, that he should be a party to such an adventure; allow such things to be done as might be done because he himself was held captive by a passion. In that minute he knew that he would have sacrificed Elise and every other woman in the world, if only Olga had once laid upon his cheek her slim, white fingers. A party to a conspiracy, to a conspiracy, perhaps, to destroy a young life. Yes, he was that; inactive yet, but consenting, because he had inextricably wound in the thread of his life among those two other threads that at all moments became one thread until, in his bewilderment, he was part of some hideous, thrilling trinity.

A consenting party—then an active one, for Fiodor, prosecuting his suit and animate of love, still suffered enough from his physical weakness to need a helper as well as a confidant. Soon it was Hulder walked down the steep hill into the village to buy sweets which Fiodor gave to Elise, and it was Hulder went into the shop and bought cigarettes, so that Fiodor might not too much be noticed of old Treitzen as he sat in the back room, peacefully smoking his long porcelain pipe. It was Hulder who whispered to Elise the hour of the assignation which Fiodor made for the day in the fields on the road to Starnois. All through he was conscious of something abominable in his role. When he thought more coolly of it he saw himself as a separate figure: a tall, good-looking young man, in modish grey flannels, leaning across the counter and talking to a young girl with fair hair and rosy cheeks, who was herself another ghost. For the figure was not he, it could not be he, this assistant to an insane romance, who could look unmoved upon blushes that went as flying, rosy clouds across a milk-white skin, and be so cold and so base as not to cry out while he might, "Take care! You are in deadly peril. Draw back while you may."

And he hated himself more as the days went and he knew that he was happy in his abjection, for the happiness of Fiodor created in Olga a state of mind by which the accomplice benefited. Very near now were the fruits of his complaisance. More than ever he longed for them, and every day, because he longed for them more, he hated himself more. Through his love of the Russian girl Hulder found running a streak of hatred and fear, as if she held him by some vile magic. But though he rebelled against the spell he knew that he was glad.

He was glad even in Fiodor's happiness because a little he had a hand in it. Every day now Fiodor went to the fields on the road to Starnois. Treitzen kept no close watch upon his daughter, and so, every day in the afternoon, under the golden shower of the rays of the sun, she went quickly, a slim figure with eyes averted and a little guilty because she had a secret, to join her lover under the shadow of a big fir tree, where the rivulet that meandered towards the lake was spanned by a white bridge. There she would sit upon the short grass that the heat had charred brown, her fingers busy with some knitting, while every minute her eyes would rove, glad and a little furtive, to see whether Fiodor were coming. And every day he came, quick stepping, his cape thrown across one shoulder, his black moustache combed at a gallant angle, with his hair flying in the wind, and about his thin frame the jauntiness of a musketeer. He would throw himself upon the grass by her side, draw her hands to his face, and talk to her wildly, endlessly, of life and love, and all the things that made beauty. She spoke but little, for she did not always understand. But, as she looked deep into the fierce eyes that devoured her, she was glad. For all this whirl of words, this periphrase, these allusions to writers and philosophers unknown to her, bore towards her the same message; it did not matter to Elise what Fiodor said: his words, set together, were her Song of Songs. And when, at last, suddenly pausing in his harangue, Fiodor seized her by both arms, drew her down and kissed her lips as if he would destroy her in a caress, she was all gladness, conscious only of a desire to be all his because she loved him and had forgotten the world.

And so, gaily on. Fiodor spoke no more of anodynes for life; he needed no longer philosophy and art; for he had found love, the anodyne which contains all others. Once he even proclaimed that optimism alone made life vital. He had forgotten Schopenhauer; almost he had forgotten all those other philosophers who had so ill reconciled him with his speeding fate. Suddenly he seemed to love all things. He called the dogs upon the road to caress them; he played gentle games with Madame Pettinger's children; he allowed the old official to tell him what Bismarck would have done to the Socialists. As his life opened as a flower, a new life seemed to come into Olga. She, too, now, could be all gaiety. She had abandoned the armour of fierce reserve with which she had protected herself against a hateful world. She, too, now, hated none, despised none and, as if Hulder, because he was the accomplice, were the engineer of her brother's happiness, she bent towards him as if already she were his. And Hulder, slowly drifting, came at last to the point where he and Olga were to meet. It was night. Fiodor, content and babbling, had been put to bed early and, as a child over-excited at a party, had gone to sleep as soon as his cheek touched the pillow.

Alone, Olga and the American went out into the moonlight, passed the hotel, the villas and their lighted windows, into the wood where they could not see each other, but were conscious only of their nearness. Then into a clearing where was a bench which the crescent moon silvered. As they sat down Hulder was thrilled with memory, for he knew that upon this bench a hundred lovers had carved their interlaced initials. For a long time they did not speak, but looked into the black void of the little valley above which the crests of the hills glowed in the moonlight. Round them the silence was complete, for the cattle had been called home and stirred not in their byres. They had a sense of the everlasting, and Olga, perhaps, would not have moved; but there was in Hulder something male and restless: silently he took her hand. She did not resist. Half unconsciously he laid his arm about her shoulders, drew her to him in one wild, intoxicating moment, knew that she had not drawn away, indeed that she had come closer, laid her shoulder against his. Then, still more wonderful, that her head had fallen upon his breast and that his lips were buried in the thick, scented masses of her hair.

He spoke, hardly knew what he said, knew only that he was trying to express his longing for her; the interminable length of a waiting which had lasted so little and yet been so heavy, so torn and racked had he been by all it held. Olga did not reply, save by a contented little sound as he drew her yet closer to him, and his strained lips, descending from her hair, found her closed eyes. For some seconds they sat, close-linked, thrilled and yet languid, together.

Olga opened her eyes, looked deep into his.

"I love you," murmured Hulder. "Do you love me?"

Olga did not reply, but, with a sudden movement, flung an arm about his neck, drew his head still closer, and swiftly, violently kissed him upon the lips, filling all his body with the shiver that ran through hers, taking, in her caress, possession of him, together giving and taking.

Still linked, but less closely, they spoke.

"I'll follow you to the end of the world," said Hulder.

"Yes," whispered Olga, "follow me, follow us, love us!"

"I am yours," he said.

"And I am yours."

"Will you marry me?"

"As you wish. In free grace or in marriage, I am yours."

The words shocked and yet thrilled him. Free or bound, she was his. Incredibly, it was true. All doubts, base, incongruous, swept away, and the moon veiled the while by the night of her hair. He bent down and felt as if he were falling, interminably falling into a depth as his eyes came nearer to her open eyes and conquering, conquered, he pressed kisses upon her lips.

Chapter IX

Days of love unwinding as a feverish scroll; love, fleeting in the high airs, borne on the rosy wings of the flamingo; passion soaring on the pinions of the eagle and below, in these abysses above which none save birds can dwell, four pale servants of Zarathustra, four souls intimately linked to one another, bound by impalpable and tangled threads, joyous in conflict, suffering in unity, together welded as four fighting beasts.

It seemed to Hulder sometimes as if the weakest of the four were the keystone of that arch upon which their relations were built. Though secure in Olga's love, and though now, for him, she was all sweetness, he was conscious that, were it not for Elise, Olga would not have been his. That she loved him, he knew. Not only had she said so, but, bolder than more Western women, abler, too, perhaps, to look deep into herself, she had told him what it was made her love him.

"I like your bigness, and your strength," she had said. "And all that short-cut, fair, curly hair. Your calmness, too. What would you say if, suddenly, the Wetterspitze were to fall into the lake? "

"I don't think I should say anything," said Hulder.

"There!" Olga laughed and clapped her hands. "That's exactly what I thought you'd do."

"One day there is the Wetterspitze, and the next day it is gone. What else is there to say about it?"

"Oh, you are wonderful, wonderful, you American people. Sometimes I think you are finer even than the English: quite as strong and not so stupid."

"You don't think we lack emotion? " asked Hulder.

"No, of course not," cried Olga, "but you're not like us; you don't let it run about the gutter. You are there, with your reserves and all the strengths that you might use." Her tone became appealing. "And you will use them, these strengths, won't you—for me and Fiodor? Oh, we need you so badly, both of us, and you love Fiodor. You do, don't you?"

"Yes," said Hulder, drawing her close.

And as he did so a strange feeling came to him. She needed him, needed his strength, his calm, his resourcefulness, needed them for herself and for Fiodor. Of course she was welcome and he, too, poor creature, racked by passion and the fear of death. But, indefinably, he felt disappointed because it almost seemed as if he were not alone with Olga, as if, when together they sat in the sun, the tenuous shade of another fell across and distorted the outline of their own shadows. But he was weak and he knew it, for in this minute, when he held Olga in his arms, held her close, and was all shaken with the powerful thrill of her nearness, he forgot. Between them was no shadow now, no shadow he could perceive, and yet, even as he kissed her lips, this shadow that he could not see was indefinably about them in the form he held, in the fragrance of Olga's breath.

And now it was not only one shadow, but two shadows: a phantom couple in attitude recalling his own with Olga. He loved, was loved, and Fiodor loved, was loved. Together the loves had come about, as if twin. And Olga and Fiodor were twins, were one. An indestructible connection seemed to exist between them all, as if he had given himself to Olga who brooded over Fiodor who intolerably loved Elise: it was a preposterous, laughable House That Jack Built, the race of the torch, the flame passing from hand to hand. But then again, when such thoughts took him, pressed him against the uneasy bosom of his intellect, he thrust them away. It was not elixir that Olga poured, but narcotic.

And still the days of love went by on wings rosy as those of the flamingo. Fiodor, in pursuit of his love, had not expressed what he wanted of her: whether passion without thought or ruth, or marriage and bourgeois comfort, or unconsciously, perhaps, a remedy for unoccupied days, or perhaps even just a lie, something to make him believe that his mind was not disordered, that he truly saw the rosy wings and not the grizzly black webs of the bat. His depression had not returned. It was not a dream he lived for; he was too active, too vital. Giving his life into the custody of another, he had taken another's life into his own charge. It seemed as if he had for the first time come into the fulness of his activity. Dead were breedings and philosophies, uncertainties, vain rages and regrets. Illumined by the high-flaming star of his passion, he rode with the Valkyr. Hulder found it hard to realize that the pink and white daughter of a tradesman could be the cause of such a revolution. He had to remind himself often that the idea was more than the fact, that the object of love is far less than love itself. But soon, in the growing egoism of his own love, which made it impossible for him to trouble about aught else, he ceased to question the end and the genuineness of Fiodor's passion. As if Elise had indeed been the high-born creature, rich in thought and emotion, who should have been Fiodor's mate, he accepted her.

Once only did he descend from the pinnacle of egoism on which every true lover dwells. Accidentally, upon the shore of the lake, opposite that spot which serves as a wharf for the little sailing boats, he met Elise. For some moments he was able to consider her unobserved. She was clad in a skirt of thin white material, over which was a plaid blouse, low-cut at the neck. Rather round-faced, her head bent a little under the heavy weight of her fair tresses, she looked intently towards the lake. All of her, the slenderness not yet redeemed by maturity, the round curves of her white neck and bare arms, all this was so young that Hulder felt moving in him something tender and sorrowful. She was as a little barque setting out upon the ocean in fair weather, and ignorant of the storms to come. He went up to her, spoke. She hardly answered, so great was her embarrassment, and so great her desire to suppress her blushes, to appear very sedate, collected and grown-up. Timidly, she inquired whether Fiodor was well.

"Oh, he's quite well," said Hulder, a little guiltily. Then hurriedly, "He's always well now."

She could not govern her blushes.

"Yes," said Hulder, "he's a new man since he loves you."

Elise averted her head.

"Why do you turn your head away? Don't you love him, too?"

She did not reply, and he saw her fingers tremble.

"Don't you? " he said, impelled by a half-conscious desire to gain the truth from her, while aware that the truth mattered little: if she loved Fiodor, she went to disaster with him; if she did not love him, another disaster must come.

"Yes," she whispered.

Hulder spoke of Fiodor, of his charm, of his wild cleverness. He painted him as a weak thing animated by a fierce spirit, and Elise listened gravely for a very long time, while Hulder spoke of his friend, and of Olga, warmly, excitedly, as if something of the ambient hysteria had touched even him. All this that was happening was not common life, but some nightmare. He had with words to drug himself into a belief in its reality. Elise listened to the end. She made as if to speak, turned away. Then her soft features became resolute; she looked him full in the face.

"Oh, Monsieur Hulder!" she cried.

There was a pause and then, suddenly, there burst from her the dithyramb of her adoration. Looking beyond Hulder, she poured forth her love song. All that she had dreamt had come the little blue flower of Swiss sentiment—the learning, the philosophical bent that many a woman reveres without understanding it—and above all the youth, heart and body aflame, Lohengrin in his silver armour drawn by the swan . . .

It was pitiful, wonderful. And, out of the tenderness of this love, Hulder drew something gentle which he laid later on Olga's altar, there to be scorched by the fierce flame of her passion. That evening, as if a plot had been hatched by earth and sky, there was a thunderstorm.

While the glittering peaks of the mountains were still bathed with rose, a mauveness crept up from the valleys towards the slopes. Purple fought with red, dominated it, and in its train came grey, long streamers of cloud rising from the south slowly moving into position, capping every peak with a grey haze which slowly grew darker until, upon a background yellow as sulphur, the clouds had set as troops about to go into action. Sulphur paled to whiteness, darkened to grey, and as, under the weight of heat and clotted water, a hush fell over the country, the clouds seemed to join up into a common blackness, blotting out the sky. And then, very slowly, the greater blackness of the mountains began to merge with that of the heavens, for a thick grey shroud of rain, many miles away, was uniting air and rock.

For nearly an hour, dull against the rattle of the forked lightning as it zigzagged like streams of molten metal across the black wing of the night, came the continuous, muffled roar of the thunderclaps joining up in a terrible chorus. Sometimes the sky was naught save a sheet of flame in which the black mountains, lit up by the bolts that struck them, appeared like lace-work cut in basalt.

The three stood at Hulder's window, against which the rain swept, sometimes sharp with hail, sometimes so heavy that it might itself have been a shower of stones, and then quite solid as another pane of glass. Before them the trees struggled in the wind, bending to earth, their branches furled round them as a woman's skirts about her limbs. And once, before their eyes, flew something large and black: the roof of a shanty torn from its walls.

An intolerable excitement seized them. Standing together, Olga and Hulder clasped each other's hands, unconscious almost of Fiodor, though they had not told him their love, as if they realized that to tell him would not have affected him, that there was room in him for only one thought. Fiodor, close against the window, stared out into the black and golden fury of the storm. He murmured to himself. His mouth worked and, little by little, he became audible.

"Storm," he said. "Revenge of heaven upon earth, fouled by man—you are like a vulture settling upon Prometheus and tearing at his liver. Strike! Yes, strike again, O Storm! Strike while you may, for we fear you not, we men, we strong things of the world. For we have wit and learning, and we have love." A flash of lightning gilded his face, gave brilliance to his eyes. "Love," he cried, "ultimate, self-sufficient, self-explanatory, accountable to none! See! There goes Love flying by upon a golden chariot, drawn by black clouds harnessed with lightning! "

He was wild, he was mad. And those two who stood with him, silent, with their souls boiling within them, were they, too, wild and mad? Were all mad, or were all men so? Could, in three weeks, three creatures lose contact with the little laws and the little habits of civilization, stand stark before a storm as if spirits thereof, because in the grasp of their passions they were tossed by a greater storm?

"Are we all mad?" thought Hulder. And, swiftly, out of some deep cavern of himself, that he had not explored, came the reply—

"I don't know, and I don't care."

Fiodor had stretched his arms towards the fire-streaked night; behind him Hulder drew Olga close in a hard clasp.

Chapter X

Fiodor lay at Elise's feet. About him, the afternoon was in mid-glory. A soft, effulgent warmth rose up from the distant waters of the lake that were unruffled as a silver mirror. He lay full-length on the charred grass, stretched out upon the cape, a little languid in the heat that had made him throw open his coat. At times, with a nervous hand, he pushed away from his forehead the matted black hair that clung to his skin. But the movement was unconscious, as was also his observation of the scene: his head thrown back, he looked at Elise, at the firm whiteness of her chin and the queer shortening of her features when so seen. Elise did not look at him, save from time to time, as if by accident, when for a moment her blue eyes would plunge deep into those of Fiodor, soft, humid and conveying, without coquetry or concealment, the gentleness of a soul surviving the turbulence of its passion. More often she let them satiate themselves with all this landscape which she had known for eighteen years and for the first time saw as beautiful. She was revisiting the land of her birth with eyes opened and made new. Before her spread the flat meadows, dotted here and there by browsing sheep; beyond were yet more meadows, then little clumps of trees, hazel and birch; quite alone upon a hillock was a great copper beech that now blazed with every leaf as metal, save here and there where the purple darkness of autumn touched it.

They were alone. Far away was a small house, white up to the ground floor, then yellow and crowned with a roof of crimson tiles. And there was no sound save the distant lowing of a cow and the soft, steady breath of the wind among the light leaves of the birches.

She was oppressed, as if all this newly understood beauty were a gift too great for one who had just discovered happiness. She had never heard of abstract beauty, this little Swiss girl. Those eighteen years of hers had been spent in Treitzen's shop, at school, in the kitchen, and, more rarely, at the fair. She knew nothing, understood nothing. And now, for the first time, as Columbus setting foot on an unknown shore, she was feeling with incomprehensible intensity; her mind was in turmoil with delight. A shy delight, almost incredulous, mixed with a fear of this thing to come which she so desired; she was as a nymph fleeing from a satyr, anxious that he should overtake her, shuddering lest he might. For a moment she let rest upon her lover's face a gaze so purely adoring, so much the gaze which came into her eyes when she knelt before the Virgin, that he noticed it, became conscious of her as a woman and not as an extension of his own personality.

"What are you thinking of?" he asked, taking her hand.

"I don't know," she said, after a long pause, "except that somehow it seems to me too wonderful to be true."

He pressed the hand, laid a kiss in the firm, warm palm.

"It is wonderful," he said. "But it's true. Out of nothing and out of nowhere, little Elise, I have come because I had to find you, and because you were looking for me. Isn't that true, little Margaret of the golden plaits? "

"Yes," she said seriously, "that's true. I have been waiting. I didn't know it until you said so, and now I know. It seemed so long, so long, mon Fiodor"

"Yes, life that is so short can seem very long. It depends what you do with it, you see. Whether you make of it a great adventure that heaps fuel upon the flame and causes it to devour you more quickly, or whether you let life consume you very, very slowly. Which is the best, little Elise, do you think? "

She looked at him, uncomprehending but still adoring.

"Whichever way you like," she said.

He laughed, sat up, threw his arm about her, drew her close.

"Ah!" he cried, with the soft, low break that comes into a lover's voice when he holds his beloved. "Whichever way I will! That's well spoken, little Elise."

And for a long time, slowly, softly, as if anxious to forego no delights, he covered her face with kisses, surrounding with a necklace of caresses her firm white neck, stinging into redness her rosy cheeks, into purple her consenting lips.

"I love you," he murmured. "I have never loved anybody before, not like this. So it must be true if it's different, mustn't it, little Elise?"

"Yes," she murmured.

"I love you," he said. "We must never be parted, must we? You will follow me, will you not to the end?"

"To the end," repeated Elise, her eyes closed, understanding him not at all and yet content to love him without understanding.

For a moment, though he held her close, he forgot her.

"It is strange," he said, "this quality of love, bound up in such little things: the curve of a lip, the tilt of an eyelash, the note in a voice, or just one stray, gentle word falling like dew on a parched field, and no more. Just one thing so slight and a world born anew. That one thing missing, and the world as sour as it was. What is it? What can it be? It isn't the body only, for one can love when one's body is failing, when one is old, when one is parted by the sea, or even by the grave. No, it is more than the body, though the body be the link. Let us know it and not take the messenger for the message. Love is the discovering of the complement, the solution of the equation, the x which makes it come right. It is a concordance of discords, the thing that makes attraction complete, just as a kiss, sweet Elise, completes."

He laughed, bent over her, his lips very close to hers.

"Qu'est ce qu'un baiser? Un point rose sur l'i du verbe aimer."

He kissed her, and for a very long time they were silent.

"And so, my angel," said Fiodor, "all things are said. I love you. Do you love me?"

"Yes," said Elise simply.

"Are you ready to dare all things, suffer all things? "

She hesitated. Something puritanic or virginal rebelled in her at the last moment. She did not know whether he meant to marry her or not and, desperately, she clung to all that she had been taught; but his grey eyes laid upon her a heavy spell: what he desired, she felt, that she would do.

"Yes," she said, gripping his hand tight. "Anything you choose, Fiodor."

He clasped her to him in pure joy, but at that moment there passed through him a new impulse strangely compounded of two impulses. Now he would tell her what she must bear. Despite Nietzsche, and Machiavelli, and all those others who had made him, he thought it fair that she should know that the instincts of a gentleman survived in him philosophical culture. He could do the handsome thing even though the ridiculous. And, mixed with this old moral feeling, there was something else: a desire to test his (power, to set himself up as plague-stricken, bearer of a plague, and yet to give to his own pride the balm of a victory. That she should love him, that was well; but that she should love him dying and dangerous, that was better.

He leant over her hungrily and wished that already she knew that in every one of his kisses might lurk her own death: terrible to her, they would be sweeter to him.

"Listen," he said; "I have something to tell you."

His tone had suddenly grown so grave that she started away from him. His eyes fixed upon hers, he did not try to draw her back. Indeed, he loosed her hands, so anxious was he to offer to his pride of conquest the greatest salve; to be able to tell himself that, without the spell of contact, he had been able to hold her.

"It's something you must know," he said, "know and accept if you love me. I am young and, to you, I seem strong, perhaps fair. But as a fruit that hangs, all gold and crimson upon a branch, and bears within its breast a canker, so am I. Do you understand?"

She shook her head. She could not understand, but she could be afraid.

"I am sick," he said. "I am dying. Oh," he cried, as she leapt to her feet with convulsed face, "so are you, so are we all. But I die perhaps a little more quickly. I may perhaps live long. A little time ago I thought it would not be long. I counted days. The days—let me count them again. One hundred and eighty-three, less two months and two days, sixty-two—no, July has thirty-one sixty-three; that leaves me a hundred and twenty days. A hundred and twenty days, Elise! If that were all, would it be enough for you?"

Hands clenched upon her breast, which rose and fell with her quick breathing, she did not reply, but stared into his face, a wildness in her pupils.

"A hundred and twenty," he said again. "It's a great deal, little Elise, even if it's true. And it isn't true. It isn't true," he cried more fiercely. "It was true, perhaps, until I loved you. But now all things are changed, and I must live even though I have but one lung."

"One lung!" said Elise hoarsely. "But then—but then—"

In her fear she was almost hostile.

Fiodor's tone changed. "But then," he said, "well, you know—consumption. Yes, that's what it is; I'm consumptive. One lung has gone and the other is touched." He seemed to see her no more. "Touched, even the other, and every day the obscure travail of the tubercles continues, eating me and gnawing me, drinking my blood, sapping my breath. I'm all poisoned with it, and steeped in it. My body's on the rack." His voice rose. "And even though I love you, even though a minute ago I thought that your love could do what the doctors failed to do, now I know it more truly. Nothing can come between us. A hundred and twenty," he muttered. And then louder, "A hundred and twenty!" He looked at her. "Will you take me for a hundred and twenty days, Elise? Bear with my humours, watch over me, love me?"

Her hands came out open towards him, but he had not seen them when he added—

"And will you take your risk, Elise? Will you take poison with every one of my kisses? Will you dance with me the dance of death? Be mine here on earth, and take poison from my mouth, soon to earth come with me?"

"Fiodor!" cried the girl. And there was such a horror in her features that Fiodor's pride reared up, stung.

"Ah!" he said. "You're afraid; then you're afraid. So that's the value of your love for me! You love me young and strong, don't you, Elise but not weak! And you love me in your safety. You won't come with me into the Valley of the Shadow. Oh," he added bitterly, "it's natural enough."

"Fiodor, I don't mean—"

"No, but what do you mean? You're afraid you may catch it, you, too. Oh, it isn't wonderful. But where's the dream? You're casting me off."

"Oh, no. Oh, no, Fiodor."

"No? You're not casting me off? Then come, Elise, take me in your arms now. Come, now you know, kiss me, be my bride. Ah, you shrink, you shrink! You're not for me, after all. You fear for the roses and the lilies of your cheek. You don't want with me to pant for breath; you don't want to be shaken by a cough and see the blood pour from your lips. You don't love me."

Suddenly Elise hid her face in her hands and she began to weep. For some moments Fiodor watched her. She was all shaken with sobs that were deep, almost noiseless, and soon, between her ringers, he could see the moisture of her tears. As he looked a new gentleness and understanding pity came to him. Was it not too much to ask of this fair young creature that, even in the cause of love, she should give herself into the hands of death? Very gently he took her hands, tried to draw them away from her face. But as he did so a little shiver went through the girl. She drew back. At that moment Fiodor loosed her.

"Ah," he cried, "you shrink, you shrink from me! I mustn't touch you; you're afraid of me, of the plague-bearer. Never mind, never mind," he shouted. "A hundred and twenty! What does it matter? It won't be long. A hundred and twenty! " he screamed. And, as he turned and began to run, he cried, "A hundred and twenty—or less!"

Elise, through her wet eyes, saw him run across the meadows. As he turned when he leapt a stile once more to cry out at her the terrible figure, she saw his face, purplish, convulsed, for the last time. She saw him take his handkerchief from his pocket and, as he vanished behind the trees, she saw that, as he stumbled on, he pressed it against his mouth. For a long time she stood alone. The cold of death had come into her hands and feet; her clothing, moist with heat, seemed suddenly to have grown icy and clammy as a winding-sheet. Her ideas ceased to connect.

Fiodor had gone—but he loved her, of course he loved her and she, too—but he was ill, very ill—and she was afraid. Yes, but what did that matter? Her mind would not hold the problem. She struggled to understand, though conscious now only of irreparable loss. Suddenly the cold of her body seemed more acute and she knew only one thing, that Fiodor had gone, that she had lost him.

She gave a low cry, pressed both hands against her cheeks, took a few steps forward, a few more, quicker; then she began to run, aimlessly, as if she did not know where she went; to run with hair loose upon her shoulders, her mouth open in a scream which her strained breath would not let her utter, to run half demented across the meadows.

Chapter XI

The denser woods spread over a little hillock between the ravines all tangled with brushwood and creepers that were spattered here and there by scarlet and purple berries. Here a couple sat, silent, under a tall pine tree. Along the base of the hill wound the road towards Starnois, like a broad white ribbon shining dustily in the evening sun. Through the boughs they could see the sky slit up by the trunks into blue panels, all of them vertical and almost geometrically similar, as if Nature with an artistic hand had conceived her landscape as a decorator. And there was no sound save, on the left, the distant ringing of the bells of the church with the swollen spire.

They had, both of them, a sense of suspension, as if for a moment the earth had stopped to breathe, interrupting the swiftness of its race round the sun. About them was the silence of the pinewoods, seldom broken by the call of a bird, where there are no leaves to eddy upon the light wind and then to fall, with a dry, crackling sound, upon the corpses of their brothers. As Hulder lay at Olga's feet, his head pillowed upon her knee, he had again something of the sensation he had experienced that first time in the boat under the ogives of the willows: content, fulfilment, peace. And yet there now mixed with his beatitude something more precise, a security in his new possession, an assurance that, however tempestuous might run the course of his passion, however much as the fleeing hare it might double in its tracks, surely and irremediably it was such that at last it must reach its goal. Under his contentment lay purposefulness. This hand, which he held, with the slim, hard fingers, it was no longer something distant, something ideal almost: it was an actual thing given into his trust, and he did not doubt that he could hold it, for the hand just then did not refuse itself. Indeed, the long fingers had, little by little, wound themselves in among his own, so that in an intimate clasp the two hot, moist palms were joined. The lovers did not move, conscious that the clasp of their hands was so close that, holding, they were almost wedded, for hands can be formal and rapid in their touch, and mincing, or sportive, or cold, revengeful, challenging. But when, very closely, they are welded into one, when phalanges are intertwined so that they cannot easily be parted, when palms touch as lips, then are truly two spirits through their bodies embracing.

But at last Hulder looked up to meet the softness of Olga's eyes. She smiled. Her full, pouting mouth parted upon her small teeth; her eyes were half dreamy, half ironic, and it was in a tone where tenderness ran coupled with banter that she said—

"What are you thinking of?"

"You," said Hulder promptly.

She laughed. "Oh, what a ready lover, and what a ready speech! Is that not the answer to give a woman always?"

Still her tone was ironic, but she laid her hand upon his forehead and softly caressed his hair.

"Your hair," she murmured, "I like it. It's so short, and it tries so hard to curl, and you won't let it. You're cruel to your hair, don't you think cutting so close those tight little curls! "

"You wouldn't like me to look like a barber's block?" said Hulder.

He, too, spoke lightly, but he was all rilled with the delight of this contact, and as he spoke slowly moved his head so that her hand should come upon his neck where the hair grew close like a brush of sturdy little wires.

"You feel like a doormat," said Olga. And still, as if captured by the vigour, the hardness of the man, she continued stroking his hair, forcing it out of its natural lie, glad to feel it rebel against her hand and ultimately prevail. Hulder turned a little to look full into her face, and in that moment was oppressed by her beauty as he never had been before, for the sunshine, as it filtered through the pine needles, had gained a mauve quality that made her pallor radiant. And something more contented him: her restfulness and her power and the response which he felt in the hand that caressed him.

"I love you," he murmured.

Her eyes, still serious, plunged into his.

"I love you. I adore you. Oh, it isn't only that you're beautiful—there's that, of course, though I suppose I've seen many other beautiful women. It's something else. Just you, I suppose."

"Yes, it's always just oneself when one loves. How could one explain?"

"Olga, couldn't you explain?" said Hulder, a little anxiously, as he sat up, throwing his arm about her waist. "Couldn't you?" he asked, with entreaty in his voice. "You can, better than I, you know."

Very close to him, she looked into his face. He could see little details of her, varying colour in her pupils, the close grain of her skin, and the faint dark down upon her upper lip.

"Explain," she said vaguely, and her brows puckered as if she were seeking words. "No, I suppose 1 can't. How can one? Just a consciousness of your presence in a world which was different before; only like that."

Hulder was moved for a moment to discuss love and self-expression, but the rhythmic rise and fall of her body against his seemed to deprive him of coherence. He did not want to argue—he wanted to know; and, in his desire, he was willing to skip all intervening steps, explanations, qualifications, possibilities. All that he wanted was to know that she loved him, to be sure of it, and then to be told it as a tribute, and again to be told it as a mere delight, and again to be told it, and again, because the love song is to men's ears the music that may be to God's the music of the spheres.

"Do you love me?" he asked urgently.

She did not reply. He held her closer.

"Do you love me?" he repeated. "Say you love me."

Her eyes were very close to his; he saw her lips move, but, before he could catch the whisper, she had come closer, laid her mouth upon his, and the discontent that was in him, that baulked desire to know, to hear, all this was swamped in the close, powerful clinging of her lips as she held him, and, as the shiver of her frame communicated itself to his, his intelligence was swamped by his emotion. To know, to understand, what did all that matter, with this shining, fragrant creature in his arms?

They had broken their link now and sat side by side, still silent, watching in the meadow below the shadow of an elm that slowly grew longer. Then Olga spoke, irrelevantly—

"How still it is. There's nobody here."

"No, nobody," said Hulder. And, as he spoke, far away upon the white ribbon of the road, he saw a figure, no more than a dark dot. Idly he watched it for a time, telling himself that it mattered little who it was, for the road passed below the hillock towards Ammenzell; nobody that walked that way could see them if they did not so wish, and yet he watched that figure growing before his eyes with an interest that seemed abnormal when taken in a stranger. It was as if some instinct bade him keep his eyes fixed upon it, or as if he were moved by some peculiarity of it. Already, when he could see that it was a woman, two things struck him. One that her course was not direct, that she zigzagged across the road. He wondered whether she was drunk, and then remembered that he was in Switzerland, where those things did not happen. The other was that the woman grew in size at a rate incompatible with walking speed. He realized that she was running, running upon the road very fast, and also from side to side, as if driven by something terrible and imperious which almost deprived her of control of her movements. Then, in the light, he saw shining a strand of fair hair, and, quite suddenly, before he recognized her, his heart began to beat as if a suspicion of something secret but sinister were upon him. In that second he knew that this was Elise running towards them—and she was alone. Could it be—

He heard a hoarse exclamation. Olga, too, had seen, recognized, understood.

"Look! "she cried. "Who's that? Elise! I'm sure it is but why is she alone? Running, see how she runs! But—but—she went with Fiodor!"

Olga leapt to her feet, seemingly unconscious of the grip which the American still maintained upon her hand. Looking away towards Elise, who was now some two hundred yards away, she seemed rigid, was, with one arm outstretched, as a statue depicted in the midst of an arrested movement; but, suddenly, her features leapt into activity.

"Look!" she cried. "Look at her face! She sways—and her hair is upon her shoulders. Something has happened; something's happened to Fiodor!"

She tore her hand from Hulder's grasp and then, with a heart like a balloon tugging at its ropes, he was running behind her down the steep towards the road. As they reached it Elise came abreast of them.

The girl did not seem to see them. Her blue eyes were staring from her face, now covered with sweat and dust; her mouth was open and twisted as if she could hardly draw a breath, and both her hands were pressed upon her breast; she was still running swiftly, one of her shoes loose and clattering on the road. She would have passed them, so intent was the gaze she bent upon the unknown goal towards which she ran, towards which she would run until her limbs gave way beneath her, or something material stopped her.

Olga thrust out her hand, seized the girl by the wrist so roughly that, carried by her own momentum, Elise swung almost round her, fell against her. But, before Elise could clasp the body that was friendly because it was human, because so badly she needed something to touch and to hold, Olga had thrust her away with a furious push, was screaming at her questions: Where was Fiodor? What had she done with him?

Elise did not reply. She stood, her eyes staring, unable to speak, and swinging from foot to foot as if about to fall. Hulder caught her in his arms, into which she fell, quite limply. She was half fainting; her head fell back upon his shoulder and suddenly she became quite heavy in his arms. He drew her to the side of the road, seated her upon the grass, her back against a heap of stones, and then, for some minutes, Hulder tended her, wiping her face, softly patting her hands. Crouching over them, her hands upon her knees, Olga again and again repeated her questions.

It was several minutes before Elise could speak, for there was no brook or pond from which water could be taken to revive her, and even then, when her body had regained energy, there was still in her mind something wild and strained, some inability to understand that which she knew. At last only, in reply to Olga, did she say—

"Fiodor—I don't know."

"But you were with him," cried Olga. "Where is he? You were with him."

"Yes," said Elise. "I was with him."

"But where is he?" Olga stamped as she spoke, and her teeth set in her lower lip.

"He ran away," said Elise, in a low voice.

"Ran away? What do you mean? Why did he run away? Where to? Where is he?"

"I don't know where he is," said Elise, and her head fell back upon Hulder's breast as if she were near fainting. But, quite suddenly, relief came. Two large tears formed in the corners of her eyes, slowly rolled down her cheeks; then more tears, coming one after the other, flooding, as if she could not control them, as if her eyes were dissolving into tears. Olga stood silent and rigid before her, realizing that nothing could be done just then, while Hulder very softly rocked the girl in his arms, murmured comforting little words and, from time to time, wiped away the tears until at last they became less violent, until Elise opened her eyes and showed by the clearness of her gaze that once more her thoughts were sequent.

"Fiodor—" she murmured. "Oh—I remember now. He ran away there across the meadows he ran away, but I don't quite know but he told me that he loved me, and he said"—her face contracted—"oh, dreadful things that he was consumptive that he was going to die in a hundred and twenty days—"

"Hush!" said Hulder, for a low cry had escaped Olga.

"It was dreadful it was dreadful!" murmured Elise. "He asked me to love him like that for a hundred and twenty days—"

"And you refused," muttered Olga, bending down.

"I was frightened, I was so frightened," whispered Elise. "He said, I, too, I, too, perhaps I would die if I married him. And he knew it. He said I was frightened; that's why he ran away." She flung both arms about Hulder's neck, hid her face upon his breast. "Oh, I'm afraid," she cried. "Hold me close. He ran away—his eyes were staring and his hair had fallen on his face."

"Back at once!" Olga shouted. She seized Elise by the wrist, dragged her to her feet, and now she was urging the two along the road. "At once, at once. We must find him. Where did he go? Speak, fool. Didn't you see?"

Elise shook her head as she stumbled on. "I don't remember; I was afraid."

"Afraid?" said Olga bitterly. " Afraid of the king of men! Little fool! Can't you even tell whether he went to the right or left?"

Elise shook her head and again began to weep.

"Let her alone, Olga," said Hulder; "she can't tell you anything. We must go back to the hotel and wait."

"Wait!" shouted Olga, and raised into the air a clenched fist. "Wait! It'll make me mad to wait."

They were walking swiftly upon the road now, and the first villas of Ammenzell were past. Still supporting Elise, Hulder held Olga's arm above the elbow as if to restrain her. She did not seem to notice it, but walked on, swinging her other arm, muttering under her breath. As Hulder walked on between these two distraught women, he, too, was haunted by a vision of Fiodor fleeing in his despair, disappointed in his love, hopeless of a doomed life, and ending it in the lake. He did not know what this meant to him, but as he felt in his own the quivering of Olga's arm, he knew that all this was not without influence upon his fate. And now, as they turned past the Royal, affronting the curious eyes of the people of the town who knew Elise well, he was hatefully conscious that he had a share in a public scene. Mixed in with his anxiety for his friend, with the pain that rilled the woman he loved, with his pity for the poor weeping child whom he led, was the self-effacing gentleman's hatred of a conspicuous position; and, as he realized this, he hated himself, called himself a bloodless, vain creature, unfit for the stress of life. Yet he was, with Elise, pushed rather than led to Treitzen's shop. He sped with Olga up the road towards the National. Once again, as on that day when they had been too long upon the lake, Olga walked swiftly, tried to run, but this time a greater fear was behind them, touched them with the spur, for it was precise now, not indefinite. They did not speak nor touch each other as they went. There was nothing they could say, for the anxiety which held them was too gnawing to need expression. They were, both of them, wildly rolling in the same area of disturbance, as two ships together sucked into the maelstrom; they needed no words.

Together they ran up the steps of the National, through the empty garden. Together, on the stairs, in hoarse voices, they called Fiodor's name, then ran into the bedrooms. There was no reply. Fiodor had not come back. For two hours Hulder had to struggle against something in Olga which he thought to be growing madness. A little of that madness was in him, too, for when he tried to reassure her, to make her believe that after an hour in the fields Fiodor would return needing her, he found that he himself did not believe this, that he had vague visions of something horrible that had just happened, which were not less terrible because they were vague. All that could be done was done. Hulder went downstairs to telephone the police officer, and sent out on a search, to which he attached a reward, several labourers from a neighbouring farm. He returned to find Olga, face down upon the bed, silent, rigid, and when he took her in his arms she still so remained, eyes closed and mouth compressed. He caressed her cheeks, and she did not resist; softly kissed her as a mother comforting her child. Again he was optimistic against the growing certainty of disaster. He told her what he had done.

"A search," she murmured vaguely. "Yes, that's good. I must go. I must search, too."

Hulder restrained her by force. "No, no, you can't go—"

"Let me go," she cried, struggling with him. But the American held her.

"No, you can't go. If he comes back here he will need you. You must wait."

"Yes," said Olga quietly. "He'll need me; I must wait."

And so they remained together silent for another hour, until the sun, dipping low, stained the sky blood-red. The room was half in darkness. There was a tap at the door.

"Entrez!" cried Hulder. A maid, open-mouthed, white-faced, handed Olga an open telegram addressed "National." For a moment she held it out at arm's length before her eyes. There was not a twitch in her features, nor did she say a word, but her face had set into a mask, dirty yellow in colour, from which her lips protruded dark brown. In that second of silence Hulder knew that Fiodor was dead and, in his horror, he, too, felt his features setting, grow rigid and so hard that, had he wanted to, he could not have spoken. Almost unconsciously he stood up, went to Olga's side, took the hand that held the telegram. She did not seem to know that he was touching her, but still remained staring at the telegram upon which Hulder, without conscious intention, read the words—

Young foreigner found shot lamp depot Gare de Cornavin. Envelope in pocket name Nazimov. Proprietor communicate police and identify body.

When the silence had lasted so long that from it spectral voices seemed to come and engage him in converse, Hulder, recovering from the horror of the shock, was all swamped with pity. Gently he tried to draw Olga into his arms, and found it was an effort to bend back her arm. Literally she seemed turned to stone, but still she gave way without looking at him, let him take her into his arms, seat her upon the bed, kiss her cheek.

"Olga," he murmured. "My poor, sweet Olga. This is terrible, but you must be brave; my darling, have courage." And then, with the egotism of a lover, that egotism which convinces him who loves that he is all-sufficient in the world, he added, "I am here with you."

Olga did not reply. Still she remained staring straight in front of her, as if her eyes could still see the words written on the telegram which she had unconsciously crushed in her hand. And Hulder, while he wondered what he could do or say, feeling that the comfort he might offer availed little against such despair, seemed to see again unrolling before him the immense tragedy of a few weeks. This was the twenty-fourth. On the first day of August he had met Fiodor. In twenty-three days he had known love and friendship; Olga and Fiodor had loved; Fiodor had died. Truly their lives had sped more swiftly than the globe which bore them.

But now Olga's silence frightened him; she was quite motionless in his arms and, when he bent down to kiss her lips, which were dry and burning, she did not respond to the caress; she seemed unaware of it.

"What are you going to do, Olga?" asked Hulder.

There was no reply.

"Would you like me to go to the station and—and do what needs to be done?"

Still no reply.

"Or," he said, with hesitation, "would you like to go to Fiodor?"

Olga's eyelids fluttered. She looked at him as if her brother's name had touched in her some chord that at once responded.

"Fiodor," she said. Then, with queer, quick childishness, "Fiodor. Oh, well, he's at Geneva. I must go to him. I must go to him now." She smiled. "I'm going to see Fiodor. How nice!"

She freed herself, rose to her feet. "Where is my powder puff?" She laughed. "How things get lost in hotels! And my handkerchief—I have lost my handkerchief."

"Olga!" cried the American, and did not know there could be such fear in his voice.

She paid no attention to him, took up her hat from the bed and put it on.

"Such an ugly hat," she said. "Look how knocked about it is, and Fiodor hates me when I'm untidy." And then, stridently, in continuous peals, she began to laugh, hands upon her hips, rocking to and fro as if swayed by uncontrollable merriment, to laugh on a shrill, high note.

The laughter seemed to pierce Hulder's eardrums, and in that minute he was almost sure that she had lost her reason. Dominating his fear, he seized her by the shoulders and, in his excitement, shook her until her head rocked backward and forward.

"Olga!" he shouted. "Don't you understand? Fiodor is dead."

As if she had been struck dumb, the laughter stopped.

"Dead," she said softly. "Oh, yes, I must go to him."

She had not shed a tear, and now she seemed quite reasonable, so reasonable that Hulder thought it best to offer no comfort.

"Shall I come with you?" he said.

"Come with me?" she replied, as if some hotel guest were offering her a polite attention. "Oh, don't trouble; why should you come?"

"But I—I" murmured Hulder.

"You?" said Olga. "Who are you?"

For a moment Hulder was silent, and a thin streak of understanding entered his mind.

"I?" he said. "Don't you know me, Olga? I'm John Hulder. You're going to marry me soon. I was Fiodor's friend."

"Oh, yes," she said, "Fiodor's friend. I remember now. But Fiodor is dead; you have no friend."

He seized her hand. "But I have you, Olga, my darling."

Gently she freed her hand.

"But don't you understand? You were Fiodor's friend and he is dead. That's all, isn't it?"

Moved by some terrible premonition, he threw his arms about her, kissed her on the mouth. For a second she submitted to the caress, then suddenly thrust him back. Her voice rose to a cry: "Who are you? I don't know you. Let me go! I say, let me go!"

She put her hand to his chin, thrust him away, ran to the door. "I'm going to Geneva! " she shouted. "Let me go!" she screamed again, as if she were being held. "I must go to Geneva, now."

Hulder ran down the stairs, conscious only, in the turmoil of his mind, that he must follow her, but she was winged with despair. Already she had fled through the front garden; he could hear her running upon the road. He was gaining upon her, already her footsteps sounded louder. Then he lost them. He realized that she must have taken the short cut on the right, down the steep little path that ran from the brewery. Stumbling in the darkness of the plantation, he followed her, but heard her footsteps no more. He must have been wrong, he thought. He retraced his footsteps, but he had lost her, and when, a quarter of an hour later, he arrived at Ammenzell, he was told that, a minute before, Olga had hired the motor-car at the Royal and driven away to Geneva. The suicide was known in the town, and Hulder found himself the object of curiosity as an associate of the dead. But he paid no attention to questions and condolences; as he walked to Treitzen's shop to tell Elise the truth in case she had not heard it, there was but one thought in his mind: he had been told at the Royal that Olga was not crying, but that she seemed filled with an ungovernable rage, that she had abused the proprietor and the chauffeur, called the latter by names which no lady would use. Except, added the proprietor, under the stress of emotion.

Hulder could not understand. Olga weeping, Olga prostrate, that would have been natural, but Olga blaspheming, raging at fate—this was something he could not grasp. He knew only that he was in contact with a temperament the reactions of which he could not understand, and it added to his anxiety and his pain that the thread of his life should have become entangled with some other strand that threatened to make of it something he could no longer follow.

Elise, at least, gave him the satisfaction of her greater obviousness. She already knew, had been told, and her father allowed him to see her for a few minutes. While Hulder knelt by the side of the girl's bed, where she lay, still white-faced and quite exhausted, Treitzen, who did not understand, stood in a corner of the room, his large pink cheeks shaken by sobs, and his good-humoured eyes swollen with the tears that his daughter's incomprehensible misery had called up. Elise did not reply to the words of comfort which Hulder mechanically gave her, nor did she weep. She was too exhausted. At last only did she murmur—

"I must go to him. I must see him once more."

"Yes," said Hulder gently. "You shall, Elise; you shall."

"Take me with you now," she said.

" No, not now; to-morrow. I'll take you to-morrow."

"No, no," she cried, more shrilly, clasping both his hands. "Now! To-night!"

She tried to sit up in her bed, but Hulder easily forced her back upon the pillow.

"No; you must be reasonable, you must rest. Tomorrow morning, I promise you there, do you hear?—I promise you, to-morrow morning."

Elise did not reply. As a child she was controlled. Besides, her weariness was such that a command from another served her as a will. As Hulder tiptoed out of the room he saw that her cheek lay on the pillow, and that her features were relaxing. In another minute, as an exhausted child, she would be asleep.

Alone he went to the station. In three-quarters of an hour he was at Geneva. From the station he was sent to the police office, thence to the mortuary. But it was nine o'clock; the mortuary was closed. The custodian said he must come in the morning.

"But I want to see him now," cried the American.

He did not know why he wanted to see his friend. Perhaps, he thought, by some mysterious means Olga had gained access to him.

"Oh, you all say that," replied the official. "There was a young lady here an hour ago; she, too, wanted to see him. I told her to come to-morrow morning. It is the rule."

So Olga had come. A brief description and a coin drew confirmation of this.

"She made a nice row," said the man. "Had to have her taken away by the police. Ridiculous, I call it."

Taken away by the police! Hulder dominated his pain, for the desire was still in him.

"I'd like to see him to-night," said Hulder, taking some silver from his pocket.

The official shook his head.

"Impossible. It is the rule. Besides," he added, half smiling, "you'll find him all right in the morning. Il vous attendra!"

As Hulder walked away, the brutal jest echoed in his head. No, Fiodor wouldn't run away. For two hours he searched Geneva, though he knew that his chance of rinding Olga was small. He thought of inquiring at the hotels, but there were hundreds of them, and, besides, who could say what Olga had done? At eleven o'clock he suddenly realized he had had no food for ten hours. He ate hurriedly, standing up at the station buffet. In another hour he was at the National, upon his balcony. Olga had not returned. And when at dawn at last he threw himself upon his bed, haunted by anxieties, horrible, incomprehensible intimations of personal disaster, she was still missing.

Chapter XII

When, next morning, the doors of the mortuary opened, Hulder stood waiting with Fiodor's beloved. The girl had been dressed in black by her conventional father. She was not weeping, and on the journey had not said a word. In fact, only once altogether had she broken silence, and that was when passing a florist's she asked Hulder to buy some white flowers. It was bearing in her arms a great bunch of lilies that she entered the chamber of the dead. As Hulder looked upon the face of his friend, 'for a moment 'he forgot the preoccupation which had been rilling him: Olga's disappearance and her attitude to him.

The mortuary was a small room, painted brownish green. There were four inclined stone slabs upon which trickled a little water. Three of the slabs were empty; on the fourth lay Fiodor. His face had not changed; it was much as in life: yellowish, a little drawn. The lips were parted, showing the beautiful teeth. And, as if nature had given way before death, or as if death had been decent, the mass of black hair that in life hung over his left eyebrow had fallen over the right so as to hide the bullet hole in the temple.

For some moments those two stood silently before the body. They had, both of them, been too racked to feel much emotion. There was no sound save in the corner the clicking of the mortuary keeper's keys as he watched the scene with an air of boredom.

"That's the gentleman, isn't it?"

"Yes," said Hulder.

"Oh, you'll have to sign to identify in the office." He nodded towards the door, then stifled a yawn.

Elise drew nearer to the body, bent down, recoiled for an instant as if afraid, bent down again and softly kissed the dead man's forehead. Then, with uncertain hands, she spread the lilies over the body, lilies upon his breast, and lilies by his side. She stopped; there was a catch in her breath; she repressed a sob, bent down to arrange about Fiodor's head a crown of lilies. As she did so Hulder heard the opening of a door, a sound—and then another sound.

"Ah! ah!" cried the voice. "Lilies—lillies—how funny!"

He turned. Olga stood in the doorway, her hands clasped together, hatless, her hair matted and falling over her face. But her eyes were not wild; they seemed clear and purposeful.

"Lilies!" she cried. "Like lace on a wound. You've come in good time, little fool, with your lilies."

She came closer to Elise, stood face to face with her.

"So you've come to see what you've done?" she said. Her voice was very low and distinct. "You've come to see the man you've killed because you didn't love him? "

Elise started back, frightened, her hands outspread as if to defend herself.

"Because you didn't love him," repeated Olga, still in low tones.

"Oh, I did, I did," moaned Elise, "only—

"Only you were afraid only you were a coward because you were ready to play with him and deceive him—and betray him—because you were willing to make his wretched life a greater hell."

"Oh, no, no!"

"Yes, yes!" cried Olga, louder. "Miserable little fool! Did you not then know how proud you should have been—that he should turn to you—oh, such a man to such a one as you! It was like the sun shining upon a weed, and you ruined him, and you killed him; but for you he would have lived. How dared you do such a thing? How dared you be such a fool? "

She took a quick step forward. Elise recoiled.

"Coward!" shouted Olga, and then again, "Coward!"

Before Hulder could move Olga had suddenly swung her arm back, and in the same movement, with the full weight of arm and body, struck Elise upon the cheek so terrible a blow that the girl reeled back and would have fallen if she had not encountered the wall. And there, for some moments, while Hulder seized Olga from behind, she remained, trembling, her hands against her mouth, and upon her cheek the purplish mark of four fingers.

"Olga! Olga!" cried Hulder desperately.

Through all his sorrow there ran again a conventional feeling: that one should not wrangle in the chamber of death. But, as he touched her, suddenly Olga freed herself.

"Don't touch me!" she cried. "How dare you touch me? I don't know you. Leave me alone, all of you."

She made a movement with both arms as if to sweep the room clear.

"But, Olga!" cried Hulder. In that moment he forgot that others heard him. "I love you. Don't you remember? And you love me."

There was a long pause. Then Olga spoke quite quietly

"Love you? I never loved you. Oh, no, perhaps I did love you, but Fiodor was alive then. He wanted you, needed you. But now he is dead. Don't you see what a difference that makes?"

"Olga, I beg you—"

"But don't you understand? He is dead; it is all different now. I can't see you any more; you are no longer there."

And Hulder, as he heard the low voice speaking philosophical abstractions, suddenly had a horrible thrill as if it were the dead man who had spoken. But energy had come into Olga. She shouted

"Go away, all of you! All of you—now!" She seized the flowers. "Take away your lilies, all of you—and go." She seized Elise by the arm, dragged her to the door. "Go, little coward, before I kill you. And you, too," she cried, seizing Hulder. And with sudden, irresistible strength, driving them towards the door—

"Go away, all of you, and leave me with my dead."

Bewildered, they stood in the corridor. The official was with them, still jingling his keys. He nodded towards a little window.

"You can see through there," he said.

Hulder bent towards the pane. Upon her knees by the side of the stone slab was Olga. Bathed in the reflected greenish light, her hands and neck had assumed the colour of the corpse's features. She knelt, quite motionless, her lax hands upon Fiodor's breast, her eyes hidden in his cape. There w r as no movement in her as she communed with her dead.

Then, little by little, Hulder found that the official was urging him with Elise towards the identification bureau. A register was opened before him. Mechanically he signed. As he did so, he heard the custodian's voice coming from some far-away region where lay shattered the dream of love, the hopes, the ambitions and the desires, all the sweetness of life ground into powder by death. He did not know what the man was saying; he seemed to be talking a great deal. Hulder knew that all was over, that between him and Olga there had never been anything save the bridge that Fiodor built. And now Fiodor lay upon the stone slab; the bridge was broken. Between him and Olga was a chasm across which never more could a bridge be thrown. Oh, what was that the custodian was saying?

"Lord! The young lady did make a fuss! They do now and then."

He yawned.

W. L. George — A Concise Bibliography

Engines of Social Progress (1907)
France in the Twentieth Century (1908)
Labour and Housing at Port Sunlight (1909)
A Bed of Roses (1911)

City of Light: A Novel of Modern Paris (1912)
Woman and To-morrow (1913)
Israel Kalisch (1913) (In the USA as 'Until the Day Break')
The Making of an Englishman (1914) (Reissued in 1916 as 'The Little Beloved')
The Second Blooming (1914)
Dramatic Actualities (1914)
Olga Nazimov & Other Stories (1915)
Anatole France (1915)
The Intelligence of Woman (1916)
The Strangers' Wedding, Or the Comedy of a Romantic (1916)
A Novelist on Novels (1918) (In the USA as 'Literary Chapters')
Blind Alley (1919)
Eddies of the Day (1919)
Caliban (1920)
The Confession of Ursula Trent (1921) (In the USA as 'Ursula Trent')
A London Mosaic (1921) with illustrations Philippe Forbes-Robertson.
Hail Columbia! Random Impressions of A Conservative English Radical (1921)
The Stiff Lip (1922) (In the USA as 'Her Unwelcome Husband' 1922. Reissued as 'One of the Guilty' 1923)
The Triumph of Gallio (1924)
The Story of Woman (1925)
Historic Lovers (1925)
Children of the Morning (1926)
Gifts of Sheba (1926)
The Ordeal of Monica Mary (1927)
The Selected Short Stories of W. L. George (1927)